"I'm not easy to match, and I know it.

"My sister is a matchmaker and even she had trouble with me. Maybe it's why I want to drag some *Englishers* into our midst."

Mose's stomach dropped.

"T-to marry?" he asked.

"No!" Naomi rolled her eyes. "But next to a bunch of *Englishers*, I'm downright safe, you know?"

"Yah." He wasn't so fortunate, though. Standing him next to *Englishers* wouldn't fix what made him different.

"I'm joking, of course. I don't think I'm actually so different from the other women—I just don't hide things as well!"

"That's…a blessing," he said. At least she was honest.

"We're polar opposites, you and me, Mose. I talk too fast, and you aren't able to say everything in your head."

Mose met her gaze. "It's h-hard being d-d-different."

"Amen to that," she murmured, then she smiled. "But a good friend helps."

Yah, a good friend did help. With Naomi and her wild hair and even wilder way of thinking, he didn't feel so alone—she'd always had that effect on him.

Patricia Johns is a *Publishers Weekly* bestselling author who writes from Alberta, Canada. She has her Hon. BA in English literature and currently writes for Harlequin's Love Inspired and Heartwarming lines. She also writes Amish romance for Kensington Books. You can find her at patriciajohns.com.

Books by Patricia Johns

Love Inspired

Amish Country Matches

The Amish Matchmaking Dilemma

Redemption's Amish Legacies

The Nanny's Amish Family
A Precious Christmas Gift
Wife on His Doorstep
Snowbound with the Amish Bachelor
Blended Amish Blessings
The Amish Matchmaker's Choice

Montana Twins

Her Cowboy's Twin Blessings
Her Twins' Cowboy Dad
A Rancher to Remember

Harlequin Heartwarming

Amish Country Haven

A Deputy in Amish Country

Visit the Author Profile page at LoveInspired.com for more titles.

The Amish Matchmaking Dilemma

Patricia Johns

LOVE INSPIRED
INSPIRATIONAL ROMANCE

LOVE INSPIRED®
INSPIRATIONAL ROMANCE

ISBN-13: 978-1-335-58518-9

The Amish Matchmaking Dilemma

Copyright © 2022 by Patricia Johns

Recycling programs
for this product may
not exist in your area.

This is a work of fiction. Names, characters, places and incidents are either the
product of the author's imagination or are used fictitiously. Any resemblance
to actual persons, living or dead, businesses, companies, events or locales is
entirely coincidental.

For questions and comments about the quality of this book, please contact us
at CustomerService@Harlequin.com.

Love Inspired
22 Adelaide St. West, 41st Floor
Toronto, Ontario M5H 4E3, Canada
www.LoveInspired.com

Printed in U.S.A.

The words of a man's mouth are as deep waters,
and the wellspring of wisdom
as a flowing brook.
—*Proverbs* 18:4

To my husband and son.
You are my reason for everything. I love you!

Chapter One

"We have a wonderful selection of Amish treats for you to sample." Naomi Peachy gestured to the assortment awaiting the *Englisher* tourists on the wooden kitchen table. "We have four different pies— peach, oatmeal molasses, shoofly pie and lemon meringue. There are a variety of cookies made by local women as well. We're also selling jars of our own jams and jellies, and our always-popular Amish peanut butter. If you haven't tried it, you're missing out! It's very sweet, but an absolute favorite among Amish people, old and young."

The kitchen of the Draschel Bed and Breakfast, which was named after Naomi's sister's first husband— it was a place with history—was spotless. Not a crumb on a counter, not a dish towel out of place. The solid kitchen table held the baked goods, neat stacks of jam and peanut butter jars, and a pile of plates and forks. Naomi Peachy and Claire Glick ran the establishment together for Naomi's sister, Adel, who owned it.

"Oh, and before you leave, we also have some crocheted items for sale in the sitting room," Claire said.

"They're made by our dear Amish friend Lydia. There are also some knitted scarves and mittens made by Naomi's own sister Adel. I'll make sure to show you after you're finished eating."

"Is any of this gluten-free?" one woman asked hopefully.

"We have one gluten-free pie over on the counter," Naomi said with a smile. "It's blueberry—my personal favorite. It was made by a young lady with celiac disease in our community, so you can be sure that it's well and truly free of gluten. She doesn't play with such things. And all of our jams, jellies and the Amish peanut butter are naturally gluten-free."

The group of *Englishers* milled around the kitchen, looking in awe at the big black woodstove, the icebox, and the hook where an unlit kerosene lantern hung. Ordinarily, Naomi would put the lantern down on a shelf when they weren't using it, but the *Englisher* guests always enjoyed seeing exactly how the hook was used.

The women gushed over Claire's three-year-old son, Aaron, who didn't normally wear his service Sunday best, but he did for the guests to enjoy. He was wearing little broadfall pants, suspenders and a straw hat that was too big but did make him look absolutely adorable. And Aaron thoroughly enjoyed all the attention he got.

Naomi looked out the window at the wagon that had brought their guests. It was a warm day in early September, and she'd been anxiously awaiting the guests today for one reason—the driver. She and Mose Klassen had been neighbors and best friends as children. His family had since moved away from Pennsylvania and settled in Ohio, but Mose had recently returned and

Naomi's matchmaker sister was helping him to find a good wife from their community.

Adel felt she owed some of the women here in Redemption after she'd married her first matchmaking client herself, and she'd vowed that she'd find good husbands for all of the women she'd considered as possible matches for her own husband, Jake. Naomi told her over and over again that no one held her marriage to Jake against her, but Adel held to her own code.

Mose was a new matchmaking client for Adel, and he'd be doing the driving for the next couple of weeks to help out his uncle, who was recovering from gallbladder surgery. But the main reason for his visit was to have a marriage arranged for him, and Naomi was almost certain that he'd find himself married to one of Adel's single women. But Mose had a peculiar problem, and Adel had asked for Naomi's help in getting him ready for introductions.

Naomi squinted at the broad-shouldered, strong man standing next to the horses. It was hard to see the boy from her memories in the tall man outside, but it would be him. He was clean-shaven, as were all the single Amish men, and when he glanced toward the house, his expression was guarded. Was Mose not going to come inside?

He was shy—Adel had told her that much. He'd been shy when they were children, too. She'd always had to be the one to draw him out of his shell, but she'd been able to do it. It looked like she'd have go break the ice, herself.

Naomi pushed open the side door and headed outside. Mose looked up as she approached, and he blinked when he saw her, then his cheeks pinked.

"Mose!" she said with a smile. "Do you recognize me?"

"Yah." He dropped his gaze. Well, she wouldn't have recognized him in a lineup of farmers, not after all this time. He'd come a long way from the skinny, freckled boy she'd counted as her very best friend.

"You don't recognize me," she countered with a laugh. "All that's left of the ten-year-old me are the flaming red curls."

"They're…they're…they're…" His face grew redder. "Un…un—" He stopped, pressed his lips together.

"My hair is unique?" she asked, finishing the word for him.

"Yah."

There was that. She used to be a stick-thin girl with wild curls that refused to stay neatly in a braid, and now she was an ample woman in her thirties with those same wild curls that still had a way of working themselves free of her *kapp*. But back then she'd been able to get Mose talking past his stutter, and Adel was counting on her being able to do the same thing again.

"You should come inside," Naomi said. "There's pie and cookies, and I can get you a sandwich if you're hungrier than that. Come in."

Mose shook his head. He pulled his hat off, scrubbed a hand through his hair and put it back on again. "No, thank…thank…" He stopped, and this time his jaw clenched.

Her heart went out to him. He couldn't say what he wanted to say, and even though she understood what he was getting at, she couldn't imagine having her words tied up inside of her like that.

"You still have your stutter," she said.

He just shrugged.

"Adel said that she thought if you could practice talking more, it might help so that she can do some formal introductions for you," Naomi said, watching his face. "She said you agreed—that you'd practice talking more…with me. You used to talk more easily with me, if I remember right. Your stutter even got a bit better."

"Yah." It seemed to be the one word he could get out easily without the stutter.

"We do have a good number of quality single women in Redemption, you know," she said with a smile.

His answer was a rueful smile.

"We had another boy here in the community with a stutter," Naomi went on. "And I just happened to be free when they needed someone to help him practice talking and reading, and those sorts of things. So I understand the situation…a little, at least."

Mose nodded. "That's…that's…that's helpful."

"You're extra nervous right now," she said. "Because you haven't seen me in ages, and here I am accosting you like some stranger." She shot him a grin.

"M-m-maybe." He returned her smile, though.

"And if I recall, when we were *kinner*, I chattered at you nonstop, and you just trailed along after me. I'm not sure I was a very good friend," she said.

"Yah, you were," he said, and his voice was low and warm—and it came out without a single halt. She felt her own cheeks suddenly heat.

"Well, I'm glad of that," she said. "I know it's hard

talking to someone you haven't seen in so long, but I'm no one to worry about. I'm running my sister's bed-and-breakfast now that she's married to Jacob Knussli. Did you hear about him?"

"No," Mose said. "Wait..." He frowned. "*Yah*. He... he...he..." He closed his eyes and then opened them. "He jumped the...the..." He pressed his lips together again, and this time she waited for him to get the last word out. "...fence."

"*Yah*, he jumped the fence," she replied. "And his *daet* passed away before he ever came back, and then his uncle finally passed, too, leaving the farm to him, but only if he was married within six months of his uncle's passing."

Mose's eyebrows climbed.

"*Yah*. So he had to find a wife, and guess who was his matchmaker?"

"A-Adel?" Mose said.

"*Yah*, and that worked better than anyone expected, considering she's now Adel Knussli."

But Adel had also introduced him to several women in the community who had gotten their hopes up before she and Jake realized they had eyes only for each other. So Adel was determined to make it up to them.

Mose grinned, and the tension seemed to be seeping out of him, his jaw relaxing, the muscles around his eyes softening, too.

"When...was this?" he asked haltingly.

"Last summer," she replied. Her sister was now expecting her first baby.

"That's...that's...that's..." He pressed his lips together again and sucked in a breath. "Good."

"She's afraid she looks like a bad matchmaker now that she married her very first client," Naomi said. "So she's going to have to repair her professional reputation by finding you a good wife."

Mose smiled faintly. "I'm... I'm... I'm..." He stopped.

Naomi waited. He had more to say, and she'd let him get it out.

"I'm...hard...to...match." He said the words slowly and distinctly. Adel had mentioned that his stutter was going to be a problem. How could a man find a wife if he couldn't even speak his mind?

Naomi looked at his face for a moment. "How frustrating is that?"

"Very," he murmured.

"You have a bucketful more to say, don't you?"

Mose met her gaze mutely, but she could see the pent-up emotion swimming around those dark eyes.

"And you stop short, because it's all that will come out, and you only have so much time because the conversation keeps going, and you never get to say it all... probably not even a fraction of it," she said.

"Yah." He smiled faintly.

"And I'm just a chattering jay all the time." She put her hands on her ample hips. "All right. I have a deal for you."

"Oh?" Mose eyed her warily.

"With me, you're going to say your piece," she said.

"I...I...I...can't."

"It's just a matter of time," she replied. "I'll stop nattering on, and you'll take as long as it takes to say it."

"No." He looked away again, and color was back in

his face. It obviously embarrassed him to think of talking that much, but what was Naomi supposed to do, just keep talking at him?

"I know from what we learned with the teenager I was helping with that once someone is a teen or an adult, the stuttering isn't going away. It's a fact. It's something you'll have to live with. Am I right?"

"Yah."

"Well, then stop worrying about it," Naomi said. "I will never expect you to speak to me without a stutter. But we can practice enough to get your thoughts out in spite of it. Does that sound fair?"

Mose frowned slightly. *"Yah."*

"Good." She smiled up at him. "Because I'm looking forward to catching up with you, and hearing what your family has been up to since you moved away. How long are you driving the wagon for your uncle?"

"Two... Two..." He swallowed. "Two weeks."

She nodded. "It'll be nice to see more of you."

He smiled in return, this time his dark gaze catching hers. "Tell me...about you."

"Me?" Naomi shrugged. "I'm not married yet—that's the big drama, if you ask my family. Even with a matchmaker for a sister, I'm single as the day I was born."

Mose smirked. "Me...me...me, too."

"And you don't have to worry about me trying to marry you," she said, giving him a teasing smile. "You're looking for a wife, and I respect that. Matchmaking has worked well for a lot of different people, but I don't want to try it again."

"Klaus," he said.

Her face heated at the memory. Mose had a second

cousin, Klaus, from Ohio who was looking for a wife just as Mose was. He'd come to Adel, too, and Adel was certain that she'd found Naomi her husband. Naomi and Klaus had written letters back and forth a few times, and the arranged marriage was almost set. Everything was ready to go until he and Naomi had their first meeting. She'd never seen a man change so quickly. He'd nearly run out the door.

No, matchmaking was not her solution. She'd be courted the proper way or not at all. Her heart couldn't take any more embarrassing rejection like she'd just experienced.

"*Yah*, Klaus," she said. "I thought I was going to be your relative, Mose. But it didn't work out. And that's okay. My sister still found him someone."

"I'm… I'm…sorry." Mose winced. "He's a…a…" He pressed his lips together.

"It's okay—" She didn't need the sympathy. It had been embarrassing and it was now over.

Mose put a hand on her arm and fixed her with a determined look. "…a…fool!" he finally said.

"Oh." Naomi smiled, appreciating him siding with her. "Regardless, that was tough for me, and I'm still a little rattled from the experience. So I'll help Adel get you matched up to some very nice woman, and then maybe I'll be braver to try again, myself. We'll see."

"F-fair."

They were silent for a moment, and Naomi wondered what other people said about her in Mose's extended family. And what had it been about her that had turned Klaus away? Was it her strong personality? Her unruly hair? Her full figure? Or was it hearing her talk?

She'd toned herself down a lot in those letters, she had to admit. Was her true, feisty personality really that off-putting? What had Klaus seen that made him run like that? She still didn't know. Maybe she'd get brave enough to ask Mose one of these days.

"*Yah*, well, like I said, I'm running the bed-and-breakfast for Adel now," Naomi went on. "And I'm enjoying it. Claire and I are determined to grow this place. My sister started the lunches and pie-tasting trips here. Claire does basket weaving, and she's very good. We're starting up some classes for local *Englishers* in basket weaving, but I think we can do more than that."

"M-m-more?" Mose frowned.

He was reacting like the rest of the community did, and she felt a little better getting onto more familiar footing. She knew how to put her back up, at least.

"Oh, you're disagreeing with me already, aren't you?" she said with a rueful smile.

"No... No..."

"*Yah*, you are. Don't mince words with me, Mose," she replied good-naturedly. He didn't answer, but he did cross his arms over his chest, fixing his gaze on her face as she continued. "Anyway, I think we can do more. The fact is, we aren't going to make an extra dime from the Amish community. People here have homes. A few travel, *yah*, and they might stay with us, but we'll never keep a business afloat by trying to convince more Amish travelers to stay here. It's about the *Englishers*. We need them, and I have some ideas on how to attract their business by including them in some of our community activities."

Naomi let out a breath, eyeing him.

"It's...risky," he said.

"I do see some risk. But in what way are you talking about?" she asked.

"The com-com-community." And this time, Naomi was determined to let him finish. His words were halting, the stutter stopped him several times, but the thoughts came out. "It's dangerous. The *Englishers* will bring their ways. They always do. It will change things here. We need to be sheep among wolves. We need to keep the fence in place to keep our ways secure. Keeping our community to ourselves is a way of protecting the more vulnerable among us."

Naomi smiled up at him.

"What?" Mose asked, looking mildly irritated.

"You disagreed with me," she said. "At length."

"I...know."

"That's going to be absolutely necessary in a marriage."

Mose rolled his eyes.

"I'm not joking," she said.

"I have no...no...trouble dis-dis-disagreeing," he said.

Naomi laughed. "Good. Now, are you hungry? Because I can go grab you a plate, if you want. Did you want that sandwich I mentioned?"

"What kind of...of...of...sandwich?" he asked.

"Roast beef, or ham and cheese," she said.

"Ham and ch-ch—" He stopped. His jaw clenched again. Naomi met his gaze, waiting patiently. He had kind eyes, she decided. Kind, and full of pent-up thoughts and feelings that she was sure didn't get expressed very often. "Cheese," he finally got out.

Ham and cheese were the sandwiches they used to eat together, sitting on the step to her house when they were young neighbors playing the summer days away. It was endearing that he still preferred them.

"I'll be back," she said.

As she walked back toward the house, she glanced over her shoulder and found Mose watching her go with a softened look on his face.

Adel wanted him to be comfortable enough with women that she could match him up with one of the single *maidels* in their community, and Naomi could see exactly what her sister had seen.

He was sweet. And if he could just get the confidence to speak his mind, he'd make a woman here in Redemption a very handsome husband.

Just not her...because Naomi could tell already that she'd drive Mose straight up the wall. And whatever had sent Klaus for the hills would likely do the same thing for Mose. She wasn't about to embarrass herself again. And who knew? She might give him the confidence to talk like every person deserved to talk—openly and unselfconsciously. There was something about his eyes that glimmered with so much unexpressed thought and emotion that made her long to help.

Mose ran his hand down the horse's side, but his eyes followed Naomi as she disappeared back into the house. He let out a slow breath.

She was beautiful. He didn't know what he'd expected his childhood friend to look like now as a fully grown woman. Mose had asked Klaus about Naomi, and he'd had some very blunt opinions about her...or women like her, as he put it. He said she was the kind of woman who was like a runaway buggy—going pell-mell down a road, a danger to everyone.

What you need, Mose, is a quiet woman, like I found in Maria. You need a woman who's gentle and soft and listens when you talk. You need a quiet personality, or the woman will run you right over. A lifetime is a long time to go with the wrong match, Mose.

And Mose had to agree with his cousin there. Mose had a tough enough time getting his own words out of his mouth that his cousin's description of the kind of woman he needed seemed quite accurate. So, when he'd written the letter to Adel, he'd asked for just that—a quiet woman with a gentle personality. The direct opposite of Naomi, it would seem.

All the same, he hadn't expected Naomi to be quite that lovely when Adel suggested he practice conversation with her. Naomi's wild, frizzy curls were hardly any tamer, but her hair was tucked back into her *kapp*, filling it up and pushing against the limits of the silky head covering. She had a pleasantly round figure, and her creamy cheeks blushed pink easily, as if her passing emotions could be seen on her skin. And this was the woman who was supposed to make talking easier?

I think my sister would like the chance to catch up with you again, Adel had said. *I'm sure she'll remember you, and she'll appreciate the distraction.*

The implication had been that Naomi would be plain and lonesome. Was that really implied, or had he been hoping that so he'd find her easier to talk to? Because Naomi looked anything but! He never should have agreed to this… Talking to Naomi wasn't going to make loosening the words inside of him any easier. She was too pretty for that, and they weren't children anymore. He needed an old woman, maybe, or a thoughtful farmer. Not *her*.

He looked toward the house again, and he saw Naomi pass in front of the window. She looked out at him, seemed to see him looking at her, and waved. He waved back, feeling embarrassed at being caught.

His uncle Abram figured that Redemption's new matchmaker might be able to suss out a woman in need of a quiet, pious, hardworking husband. If Mose wanted to get married, he'd better at least be able to talk to some women. Because even with a quiet woman, marriages took a certain amount of talking to sort out…and to maintain. He wasn't a fool.

But the kind of woman who'd be satisfied with a husband who didn't talk much, but who worked hard, would likely be a woman who didn't talk much, either. Klaus hadn't been wrong about that. And it might help his chances if she had more character than beauty. Beautiful women could have their pick of husbands, and he wouldn't be able to compete there. He could be very happy with a woman who was good to him, who cared about him, and didn't expect him to be overly charming. He could see deeper, past a woman's superficial appearances to the heart within, and he needed a woman who could look past his stutter to his heart, too.

The side door opened and Naomi came back outside, a plate in one hand and a tall glass of lemonade in the other. She walked down the steps cautiously and then headed in his direction. When her green gaze glittered with a smile, his heart skipped a beat.

"Here you are," she said, handing him the glass of lemonade first. He accepted it and took a couple of gulps. It was hot out, and he was thirsty.

There was the promised ham and cheese sandwich on the plate, a pickle spear on the side. He put the glass down on the ground next to him and picked up one half of the sandwich.

He held the plate out to her in a silent offer to share. Naomi picked up the other half, and they each took a bite. For a moment he chewed in silence. It was a delicious sandwich made on fresh, white bread.

"We used to have fun playing together, didn't we?" Naomi asked.

He nodded, his mouth full.

"Do you remember when we were trying to fish at the creek, and I got two leeches on my leg?" Naomi shook her head. "We couldn't get them off, and we decided they were poisonous and I was going to die."

Mose chuckled at the memory. *"Yah.* I…I…d-d-didn't think you'd die." He stuttered over the words. "That was all you."

"It was not!" she laughed, then shook her head. "Well, considering I did all the talking, maybe it was. But you played along."

"Of course," he said. "You were my…my…only friend."

She blinked, sobered. "Oh, Mose…"

"Not…anymore," he said, attempting to erase the pity in her eyes.

"It was hard for you when you were young," she said.

"Yah." He took another bite of sandwich. It was hard for him now.

"You weren't my only friend, Mose," she said. "But you were my best friend."

Mose swallowed, meeting her gaze for one heart-stopping moment. As a boy, he'd been silent. He'd just followed her around, held sticks, frogs or ladybugs when she wanted him to, and tagged along after her. And then he'd go home, and after chores were done, he'd look in the direction of the Peachy farmhouse, and he'd wonder what his friend was doing...if she'd kept the shiny rock he'd given her, or if she knew how much she meant to him.

"How?" he asked with a shake of his head.

"You listened to me chatter," she said softly. "I know I said a lot of foolishness. I just talked and talked. At home my *daet* and *mamm* kept telling me to think more and talk less. You know the verse that says, *In the multitude of words there wanteth not sin: but he that refraineth his lips is wise.* They recited that verse to me over and over again. They were right, of course, but I just couldn't do it. Everything came out of my mouth and bypassed my brain, as my *daet* used to say. And I know it was selfish—I'm an adult now, and I can see now what I never recognized as a little girl—but having a captive audience listen to me was really nice. I liked it. And thinking about it now, I'm embarrassed because you might not have said anything, but I'm sure you thought plenty. And I was very silly."

"You...you...you were fun," he said.

"*Yah?* I guess I had that," she said.

Naomi had imagination, and unlike the other children his age, she'd included him in it. She used to make up the most dramatic games, like when she got the leeches on her leg, declared them poisonous, and required Mose to drag her by her underarms back home. He hadn't been able to get more than a few yards, so she agreed to walk, but she'd made him solemnly promise that when she died, he'd visit her grave every full moon and put wildflowers on it.

And he would have, had she actually been dying. That was the part that wasn't silly. If she'd been right about her poisonous leeches, he'd have never forgotten her. Ever. Fortunately, a dose of salt on the leeches popped them right off, leaving nothing but a couple of blood smears behind.

Naomi nodded to the pickle. "I made those pickles."

"Yah?" He put the last of the sandwich into his mouth, then took a tangy bite of dill pickle. He nodded appreciatively. "Hmm…"

"I've been told my pickles are quite good," she said with a smile. "And if they aren't as tasty as I think, don't tell me. I don't want to know."

He chuckled. "They…they…are."

"You always were nice to me, Mose," she said, and she cocked her head to one side, surveying him. "So how would you like to do this conversation practice? Do you want to come for dinner tonight? We could talk more then."

"Yah." He swallowed. "I'd… I'd…" He wanted to say he'd like that very much. That he'd be honored to come have dinner with her. But all he could get out in a timely way was, *"Yah."*

She smiled. "Good. I'll cook something special. That should make up for the agony of being forced to talk at length."

Looking into her twinkling eyes, he knew it wasn't going to be quite the agony that she thought. And maybe Adel had been right after all, about getting more comfortable with expressing himself. If nothing else, Naomi did get him to talk.

"I wanted to tell you my ideas of including *Englisher* women in some sewing circles," Naomi said. "And getting some *Englisher* men to come help at barn raisings."

Mose blinked at her, and Naomi waggled a finger at him. "Aha! That's the look I expected. Prepare your arguments and come ready to talk me out of it, if you like. But I'm seriously very set on at least getting some *Englisher* and Amish craft circles. I'll tell you more about it tonight."

The door opened again and the *Englishers* came outside chatting and talking. They had jars of preserves in their hands, and a couple of women carried some of the knitted and crocheted items, too. They turned back to thank the other Amish woman effusively.

"This is just the loveliest place!" one gushed. "I'll have to bring my husband back here for our anniversary, if I can get him to go anywhere without Wi-Fi!"

The *Englishers* laughed at that, and Mose headed back to the wagon. He pulled down a box for the *Englishers* to use to get up inside, and he glanced over his shoulder to find that Naomi had gone over to Claire to help answer some questions from a young couple.

He let out a slow breath.

"Would you help me up?" an older woman asked.

He wordlessly smiled and took her hand. It was laden with rings—a wedding ring, an engagement ring, and a couple others that looked old. She'd lived a long and fruitful life, it would seem. The *Englishers* showed it with their jewelry. The Amish...they didn't show those lives so obviously. You had to know an Amish woman personally if you wanted to know the blessings of her life. Mose helped the older woman up and she beamed at him as she settled into a seat.

When the last of his riders were settled, he hoisted himself up, and when he looked toward the house again, he found Naomi's gaze locked on him.

There was no outward way to see what life had done for Naomi, or how Klaus's insult had hurt her, but he wanted to know if life had turned out well for her, after all.

"See you tonight, Mose!" she called in Pennsylvania Dutch.

"Yah!" he called back. It was the one word that would come out without a stutter, and the only one he trusted himself to say just now.

He would be back tonight, for sure and certain. He wanted to learn more about her, too. If he was going to have to open up and talk, that was only fair, wasn't it?

Chapter Two

Naomi watched as the horses pulled the creaking wagon out onto the main road and disappeared from sight. Another tourist visit complete, and everyone had seemed to enjoy themselves. It was a success, but Naomi's mind wasn't on business right now. It was on the man she'd seen again for the first time in twenty-three years.

Mose was entirely different now, of course. But she'd known he would be. Still, he was strong, solid, handsome…and he'd grown into a man of firm conviction. That was attractive, except that his convictions and hers were as different as dogs and cats.

Naomi went inside the house and she and Claire cleaned up the table. Three whole pies had been consumed, and they'd sold several jars of preserves as well as peanut butter. The tourist groups paid for the pleasure of coming to eat at their bed-and-breakfast and sample some authentic Amish baking, but every little bit of extra income helped them to keep afloat.

Claire swiped Aaron's hat off his head and put it up on a peg to keep it in one piece until the next group of guests would arrive the following day, and she passed him an extra cookie as a reward for his good behavior.

"You were a good boy, Aaron," Claire said, and she bent down and kissed his forehead.

Naomi smiled at the little boy standing proudly with a cookie clutched in one hand.

"I *was* good," he said.

"Very good," Naomi agreed. "Everyone loves to see our sweet little Aaron, don't they?"

He was too little to understand that the *Englisher* guests weren't just gushing over a sweet boy, but it was his unique culture that made him so intriguing to them. But it was the same for all of the Amish—their distinct lifestyle made them of interest. That was why *Englishers* came to visit their vegetable stands and took tours to try their baking. It was why they bought their quilts and their handmade furniture, and why they would pay for jars of jam made by Amish women instead of just buying jam in the store, or making their own if they were so keen on the homemade variety. They came to see what made the Amish so different.

Naomi didn't like that emphasis on their differences. She never had. And she was very likely the only one who didn't, because the *Englishers'* curiosity about them drove a lot of the business that kept them making enough money to keep their families. It was necessary. It was a blessing. But to Naomi, being the object of such curiosity also made her feel like they were museum pieces, or zoo animals.

And that was why she wanted to change things… just a little bit. But hers wasn't going to be a popular idea in these parts. And she'd need permission to do it.

"The *Englishers* never have much of the molasses oatmeal pie," Claire said.

"I know," Naomi replied. "But I really do want them to taste authentic food, not just food that's familiar to them. If they want to learn about us, it comes with a bit of molasses."

Claire chuckled. "*Yah*. I know. I suppose we can finish it up for dessert tonight. The driver is coming over, isn't he? Hopefully he'll come hungry."

"*Yah*, I think he will," Naomi said.

"He seems to like you," Claire said. "He didn't even come inside with the *Englishers*. He just stood out there talking to you."

"Actually, he stood out there, and I talked to him," Naomi said with a grin. "He's an old friend and he's handsome. That's all you're seeing. He hasn't seen me since I was about nine or ten, when his family moved to Ohio. His name is Mose Klassen."

"Did he know you'd be here?" Claire asked. "Or did he just stumble across you?"

"Oh, he knew." And he'd still not come to the door. She felt a pang at that. "My sister is helping him out with something, so he knew I'd be here. But he's driving for Abram for a couple of weeks."

"So Redemption's matchmaker is helping him…" Claire's eyes twinkled. "It sounds like she's helping him find a wife."

"*Yah, yah*, but I'm not the one to match him up with. So you can just stop that line of thinking, Claire Glick. You know what happened when my sister last tried to arrange a marriage for me… It was awful."

"I know. I'm sorry."

"Well, Klaus, the man who took one look at me and ran, is Mose's second cousin."

Claire's eyebrows rose. "Oh!"

Naomi carried a pie over to the counter to cover it with plastic wrap.

"Wait… Mose Klassen?" Claire frowned, then went over to the Amish newspaper and picked it up. She flipped through, then held up a page that Naomi couldn't see from where she stood but knew exactly what page it would be. "Not the same Mose Klassen from *The Budget*…"

"*Yah*, the same," Naomi said. She'd been following his column on *Ordnung* observance for the last couple of years since he'd started writing it. He had a simple, honest way of communicating the details of their faith to other Amish believers.

"I didn't know you knew him!" Claire said.

Naomi shrugged, but she felt her cheeks heat. She had kept him private. "We were friends as children. That's all."

"And friends now, it seems," Claire pointed out.

"Well…newly acquainted."

"Seriously, though," Claire said, "would you consider him…romantically?"

"You see the kinds of articles he writes for *The Budget*," Naomi said. "He's very conservative, and intelligent, and has a wonderful mind, but I wouldn't do well with a conservative farmer. I'm too free-spirited."

"Hmm."

"And his cousin ran from me! I don't know what it was about me that he hated, either. My sister won't say." Naomi shrugged. "I'm not putting myself into that kind of situation again. I'll be courted properly by a man who's actually interested. No more arrangements."

"I understand why you wouldn't want to do that again," Claire agreed. "The problem was with Klaus, not you."

"And yet I'm still single. He's married now, you know. My self-confidence has taken a hit," Naomi said. "One day, I truly believe *Gott* will bring me the right man. He made me too good a cook to not give me a man to cook for. But he'll have to be a man who doesn't want to run out screaming because of my liberal views...or whatever it was that spooked Klaus like a young horse. And trust me—Mose will be driven straight up the wall by my liberal ways. I saw it in him already."

Claire chuckled. "I do love how you see things, Naomi. And I do think *Gott* will bring the right man to eat your good cooking. *Gott* never lets a talent go to waste."

Naomi *did* pray that *Gott* would bring the right man to her. Or even fling her into the right man's path. Naomi wasn't picky about how *Gott* worked in her life, just so long as He was working.

"You have to know that Mose has a very noticeable stutter," Naomi said. "He's going to be coming here to practice chatting with someone—that's part of my sister's plan to get him ready for proper marriage discussions—and it's important that Mose feel comfortable. He's very self-conscious about it."

"Oh, that's why he's coming..." Claire sobered.

"*Yah*, that's why."

"And you said that you think you'll drive him up the

wall with your liberal ideas. What will you talk to him about so that he'll be comfortable?"

"Well...quite honestly, probably things that frustrate him," Naomi admitted. "I don't need him to agree with me. Maybe he'll be sparked into talking more just because he disagrees."

"So you'll argue with him for his own good?" A smile tickled at her friend's lips.

Naomi considered for a moment, then nodded. "If it comes down to that, I will. But he's very self-conscious about his stutter."

She found herself feeling protective of Mose all the same, just like she used to when she was a girl. Claire wiped Aaron's hand from his cookie's melted chocolate chips.

"Naomi, I've got my own little boy to attend to," Claire said, glancing up with a knowing smile. "I'm sure after dinner I will be ever so busy with him. There's bath time, and worship time, and I might even take him out for a little walk before I tuck him in tonight. Mose won't even notice I'm around."

Claire was going to make herself scarce, and while it was welcome, Naomi didn't want to make it so obvious that she wanted the kitchen to herself this evening.

"That's not what I meant," Naomi said, and now she was quite certain she was blushing.

"Your sister sent him." Claire shot her a grin. "She's got something up her sleeve. And Mose is very single. As are you..."

"As are you!" Naomi retorted, but she regretted the words immediately because she didn't want to share Mose's company...at least not right away. "But it would be nice to just catch up with him a little bit. He was my best friend when I was little. We played for hours together."

"Did you make him little pies and pretend that you were keeping his house?" Claire asked with a chuckle.

"I did not!" Naomi laughed. "I pretended I was dying of poison and made him help me plan my funeral."

"Really?" Claire rolled her eyes in good humor. "You were quite dramatic."

"I got him to explore about three miles of creek with me, too," she said. "I wanted to see if it ever turned into a river. It didn't."

"It does eventually," Claire said. "All creeks do. If you follow them downstream far enough."

"*Yah*, I knew that," Naomi replied. "But there is only so far two children can walk on their own before they get hungry, or wear a blister, or a neighbor sees them and sends them back home with an armload of cut flowers or a jar of jam. That's how the neighbors would make sure I went back—give me something for my mother."

"Clever." Claire looked down at her son with a wistful smile. "He'll grow up, too, one of these days, won't he?"

"Never," Naomi said, and she ruffled Aaron's curls. "He'll stay little and sweet always."

The women exchanged a smile. It was their joke—that Aaron would never grow up, and they would never grow old, and somehow everything could stay fresh and lovely always. Naomi knew it wasn't true, but it seemed to keep Claire cheerier.

"What will we make for dinner?" Claire asked.

"I have that lamb shoulder," Naomi said. "That should feed us all."

"I like lamb," Aaron said. "And mashed potatoes."

"We will mash them just for you, Aaron," Naomi said.

"Now you can run outside to play," Claire told her son. "Naomi and I have work to do. But don't go far. You stay in the yard."

"Yah, Mamm." He smiled sweetly and headed for the side door.

The women were silent for a couple of moments, and then Naomi said, "You should let my sister find you a husband, Claire. A *daet* for Aaron."

"It isn't in my future." And the sad look was back in Claire's eyes again. "I don't need a husband. I need a job to keep my son fed."

And that was what Claire always said. Was it possible that Adel had been thinking of matching Mose and Claire when she sent Mose here? Was it selfish of Naomi to feel a spark of jealousy at that thought? Naomi pushed it back with a silent prayer.

"A good man will understand about Aaron," Naomi said quietly.

"Would he, though?" Claire shook her head. "Don't worry about me. I've got a job, a roof over my head and food to feed my son. And I have a true friend in you. I'm blessed beyond measure."

"Amen," Naomi murmured. "So am I."

In so many ways. She just had to keep that fact front and center in her mind so she could be satisfied with her lot in life. She'd be the friend Mose deserved, and she wouldn't drag him along on any more of her foolish adventures. She was a grown woman now, after all. Life was no longer a game.

"Naomi Peachy has always been a little too interested in the *Englishers*," Mose's aunt Linda said as she dried a dish and put it away. Mose sat with his uncle at the table next to a pile of books, his Bible at the top of the stack.

"Now, Linda." Abram adjusted himself in his chair, still in a little bit of pain from his recent surgery.

"She has been," Linda said. "You know it's true, Abram. She's always been just a little wild. It's one of the things Klaus mentioned, too."

Wild. Mose smiled at the word. *Yah*, it did describe Naomi as a girl, for sure and certain. She'd never been a quiet, demure Amish girl. She'd been full of games and ideas and fun, and the woman he'd seen this morning still had that sparkle about her. She talked readily, and she was smart. She could roll right over him if she wanted to.

"Well…" Abram spread his hands. "She's been loyal to our community, and she's running that bed-and-breakfast for her sister. She's a wonderful cook—" Abram caught his wife's eye and paled. "Not as wonderful as you, my dear. But a competent cook, who has won contests at the fair. If you entered, Linda, you'd win, too."

"An *Englisher* fair," Linda said with a shake of her head. "And what would I do that for? To put myself above others? No. I cook for those I love. That's how it should be."

Mose hadn't heard about these things in Ohio, and

his gaze flicked between his aunt and uncle as they discussed local gossip.

"And what about that *Englisher* boy she spent so much time with during her *Rumspringa*?" Linda clucked her tongue.

"B-b-boyfriend?" Mose asked. That detail mattered to him, somehow. It shouldn't. Naomi's *Rumspringa* was a long time ago, and her relationships certainly weren't his business. Still he waited for whatever information he might glean on the subject.

"Not that she'd admit to," Linda said. "Just a good friend, she said. But come, now. At that age, spending all her time with some *Englisher* boy who'd drive her around in his pickup truck with that worldly music playing... It was a boyfriend."

"Worldly...well, it was their church music, if I recall," Abram said.

"With guitars and drums—" Linda shuddered. "Worldly, Abram."

"Now, Linda, Mose isn't going off to marry Naomi, he's going to get some practice in talking. And if he can relax enough to talk with Naomi Peachy, then he'll do quite well with other available young women who are quieter and more reserved."

"That's true..." Linda sighed. "The thing is, Mose, she's a very nice woman. I like her. I sew with her in quilting circles, and she has a good heart. She was born Amish, she lives Amish, she abides by the rules, but all the same, she's just so..."

Linda couldn't seem to find the word to describe Naomi, and the men stayed silent. Mose understood. Naomi was hard to pin down and hard to describe. There seemed to be something inside of her that grabbed hold of the bars of a cage and rattled them.

"It's why she's still single, I think," Linda said quietly. "And it's a shame, because she really can cook. A man could do worse than coming home to a meal cooked by Naomi Peachy. He'd just have to be the right man."

Abram didn't answer and fixed his gaze on his folded hands in front of him. It was probably the wisest course of action.

"I'll... I'll... I'll find out...to—" Mose closed his eyes, frustrated.

"You'll find out tonight," his aunt finished for him, casting him a fond smile. "You'll eat well, Mose. And I hope this trial by fire that Adel has in mind works to help you talk more easily. Because you deserve a wife and little ones of your own. It's time for you to settle down."

"Yah," he said. That was why he was here. He did want to settle down with a family of his own. He longed to rock a baby in his arms, to come home after a hard day at work to the scramble of little feet, and to a wife's warm embrace. But that couldn't happen if he couldn't talk to a woman long enough to get her to fall in love with him!

He pushed back his chair and tapped his watch.

"Right—" Abram looked at the clock on the wall. "You've got a tour to pick up soon. Thank you for helping me with this, Mose. The doctor said I had to take off a full two weeks, and your aunt insists that I listen to him. One more week and counting."

"I do insist," Linda said with a smile at her husband.

"You're a real blessing, Mose," Abram said.

"It's no…no…no…problem." He gave his uncle a nod. "See you lat-lat—" He cleared his throat. "See you."

Mose drove another group of tourists around the town of Redemption, stopping at shops in town, and then driving out to the country for a glimpse of Amish farms. They would head back past a popular dairy that had an ice cream shop attached. His uncle had drawn the maps for him, and it was simple enough. But as the horses' hooves clopped merrily along, his mind kept skipping back to Naomi.

Funny—he'd heard a little bit about Naomi and her family from his aunt and uncle over the years. Just information in passing—family members who had died, or were ill, marriages, babies, that sort of thing. Naomi hadn't factored into much of it, but it had been connected to her.

He'd always cared, listened for news of her, prayed for her to have a happy life. She'd taken a lonely little boy with a stutter, and she'd given him the gift of friendship. It had meant the world to him. But he'd never questioned that she'd find a good husband and settle into her life. The fact that no man had managed to marry her was surprising. She seemed to be rather liberal in her views, but she was still beautiful and fun to be around.

The *Englishers* in the wagon chattered behind him, pointing out the obvious.

"Cows! Look at them all!"

A boy attempted to moo at them, to no effect, and Mose smothered a laugh. One of the older people in the wagon told the boy that since brown eggs came from brown hens, then chocolate milk came from brown cows, and Mose almost turned around then, but he stopped himself. What was he going to do, just see if the words would come out fluently or not? It wasn't worth the bother. They'd set the boy straight eventually. They were only having fun.

"Did you see that?" a woman asked excitedly. "I see laundry on that line. It looks like sheets...wait—there's some dresses, too!"

"Do you see those pants on the other end? It's a whole family's laundry, all in a row."

"Let me get a picture!"

"Zoom in."

It was amusing to hear them so excited over everyday things. If only the women in those houses could hear the utter delight over their washing. The tourists were also enthralled with buggies, horses and some kids playing in a splash pool on the warm September day. He didn't turn around to see them taking pictures with their phones, even though he knew they'd snapped a few of his stubborn back already. He didn't encourage questions, either, and he knew he came off as unfriendly, but it was easier than trying to talk to them.

Mose waited in the wagon while they got their ice cream, and one woman came back with a vanilla soft serve cone for him that she handed over with a smile. He accepted it, feeling a twinge of guilt that he couldn't be friendlier with these people, and he ate it in silence until the wagon filled up again, and they headed back into town to end the tour. Not all the tours passed the bed-and-breakfast, unfortunately.

He was watching the time. Three thirty, four thirty,

and finally five. When he dropped off his last tourist group, he turned the wagon around and headed back out of town toward the Draschel Bed and Breakfast, which wasn't far. This was what he'd been waiting for.

He turned in the drive, and he spotted the little boy playing by the garden. He stood up and waved and Mose reined the horses in.

Mose would be staying more than a few minutes, so he started to unhitch the horses right away, and the little boy came bouncing up to him as he worked.

"Hello," he said. "Who are you?"

"I'm…M-M—" He hated this. "I'm Mose."

"How come you said it like that?"

He sighed. "Because I stutter." The words came out haltingly.

"Oh. Can you stop it?"

Mose looked down at the little boy, whose expression was entirely earnest.

"No," he said simply.

"Oh…" The boy chewed the side of his cheek. "My name's Aaron."

"Hello, Aaron." And those words came out smoothly. It was always a pleasant surprise when that happened.

"Are you coming for supper?" Aaron asked.

"Yah." He finished unhitching the first horse and walked him over to the corral.

"Naomi and *Mamm* are making lamb," Aaron said. "And mashed potatoes. And gravy."

Mose could smell the cooking from out here, and he smiled down at the boy. Aaron rubbed a hand over his forehead, leaving a dirty smear behind.

"Are you h-h-hungry?" Mose asked.

"*Yah*. I'm starving."

"Me, too."

Mose went back to the second horse and started on the buckles while Aaron watched.

"The tourist ladies like my hat and my suspenders," Aaron said, hopping from one foot to the other. "And they say I have good manners."

"That's a good thing," Mose said, the words halting again.

"And they say that I'm handsome, too," Aaron said. "But my *mamm* says I shouldn't care about being handsome so long as I have a good heart."

"Hmm," Mose said, listening to the boy chatter. He undid the last of the buckles and led the second horse toward the corral where they could eat and drink for a few hours until he hitched them back up. The horses had already worked all afternoon on the tours.

"Do ladies call *you* handsome?" Aaron asked.

Mose headed up toward the side door, Aaron in tow. "Not…not…not…often."

"But sometimes?" he asked.

Little boys were called handsome by *Englisher* ladies more often than grown men were, and it wasn't a good thing for a boy's character to be told that he was good-looking too often.

"It's not Amish," Mose said.

"Naomi calls you handsome," Aaron said. "I heard her say it."

"What?" Mose felt his face warm.

The door was open as he came up the steps, only the screen between them and the kitchen, and Naomi stood in the doorway. She pushed open the screen to welcome them inside with a smile.

"Naomi does what?" she asked, and she stepped back to let Mose inside. Her face was pink from the warm day, and he couldn't help but notice the freckles across her creamy skin as he slipped past her. He cleared his throat and shrugged.

"Oh, n-nothing," Mose said.

"You said he was handsome," Aaron said. "Like the tourist ladies say that I'm handsome. Right, Naomi? You said that he's handsome."

Naomi's face suddenly blossomed into red, and Mose couldn't help but chuckle.

"I—" She rolled her eyes. "I only said that you were no longer a little boy like I remember you, and…" She sighed. "I can't tell a lie, Mose. I did say that you were handsome."

"Yah?" Mose shot her a grin.

"Don't you let that go to your head, Mose Klassen," she said, turning her back on him and heading back into the kitchen. "I'm sure you're well aware of your own good looks. I won't be mentioning them again, I assure you."

"At least not in front of little ears," the other woman said, and she laughed when Naomi shot her a look. "Aaron, go on upstairs and wash up. And don't forget to wash your face, too." Then she gave Mose a nod. "I'm Claire Glick. I'm Naomi's employee."

"Well, more than an employee. We both live here and work the B and B," Naomi said.

He wanted to ask more questions, but they would

have come out haltingly, and he didn't want to do that in front of this other woman, so he kept his mouth shut.

"Have a seat, Mose," Naomi said. "Dinner is almost ready."

"I'm just going to help my son get washed up," Claire said. "He'll come down wet, and not actually clean."

Mose smiled faintly and nodded. Claire went up the stairs after her son, leaving Mose and Naomi alone in the kitchen. Mose watched Naomi for a moment—her rounded figure, a few stray curls springing free from her *kapp*. She was beautiful in that wild, natural way that intimidated him.

Naomi brought a bowl of mashed potatoes over to the table and set them on top of a knitted pot holder, then she met Mose's gaze and the color in her cheeks deepened again.

"I'm embarrassed," she said.

He shrugged. "D-don't be."

"Let this be a lesson to you, Mose," Naomi said, heading back toward the oven and putting on oven mitts as she went. "You may very well have all sorts of women talking about your good looks behind your back. If that doesn't give you confidence, I don't know what will."

But he'd never overheard any kind of talk like that, and right now, he wasn't overly concerned about other women's opinions of his looks. Appearances changed over time, and not normally for the better in a man's case. It wasn't a good idea to pin his hopes to things like that... If anyone else had said it, he would have brushed it off. But with Naomi?

Her cheeks were still pink. She was embarrassed still.

"Good l-looks," he stuttered, "shouldn't matter."

"Very true," she said, casting him a glance over her shoulder. "And we women would do much better to simply talk about a man's character and leave the rest alone. I wasn't saying anything too bad, Mose. I was just surprised to see what you look like as a grown man. I'm sure I'm a bit of a surprise, too."

"Yah." Except, Naomi was intimidatingly pretty.

"And you have a mirror, don't you?" She turned back to the stove. "It isn't like you aged into a billy goat or something!"

She laughed at her own joke, and he couldn't help but smile. *Yah*, with Naomi it was different. It was like when she used to tell him he was strong as a horse when he carried sticks for her to build a playhouse, or when she'd tell him he was smart, just because he'd nodded at something she'd said. With Naomi, even frivolous compliments sank a little deeper.

And she'd called him handsome.

Chapter Three

Naomi looked up at the ceiling where Aaron's laughter was filtering down. Claire was remaining true to her word about being scarce while Mose was visiting, but she didn't need to be too obviously avoiding them, either.

She looked back at Mose, who was studying the tabletop. She'd said too much. She normally did, and it was probably time she stopped treating Mose like a brother and saying things so openly.

"It…it…it…" Mose stopped.

"It…what?" Naomi asked.

"It…" He pressed his lips together for a moment. "It…smells…good." He heaved a sigh.

"Thank you. I've been cooking hard for you. I think you deserved the fatted calf, coming back like this." She shot him a smile.

"*Yah*, I… I…" He pressed his lips together, his frustration evident on his face. "Sorry. It's…h-hard."

"Don't you apologize for simply opening your mouth

and talking," Naomi said. "Everyone knows I do it often enough."

He smiled at that, and he leaned back in his chair, looking more relaxed.

"Lamb?" he asked.

"*Yah*. A shoulder roast with mint jelly, cranberry sauce, mashed potatoes, and some salad. You know, I can't get anyone else to eat salad around here. Claire doesn't like it much, Aaron won't let it past his lips. So I hardly ever make a nice tossed salad. Please tell me you like salad."

Mose's smile turned impish, then he shrugged. "*Yah*. I...like it."

"You're lying," she said with a laugh.

"I'll like yours," he said. The words were halting, but the grin was perfectly smooth. Naomi rolled her eyes.

"Don't force yourself to eat something you don't like for me." But she couldn't help but return his smile. "How are your parents?"

"Getting older," he said. Again, the words were halting, but she was getting used to it.

"That's a blessing," Naomi said. Both of her parents had passed on already.

"How are...are...your brothers and sisters?"

For the next few minutes they chatted about family, avoiding the one family member who was on both their minds—Klaus—and Naomi noticed that as Mose got more relaxed, his stutter was less pronounced. He still got stuck on some words that just wouldn't come out, and when that happened, the stutter would get much worse.

"It's okay," Naomi said. "What were you going to say?"

He just shook his head. "It's not...not...not..." She could see the frustration all over his features. "...not... worth it."

But she'd wanted to hear his stories. It was worth it to her, but she understood. Here she was making small talk, and the effort it took him to bring out the words was probably not worth the trite, polite thing he was going to say. Not for him, at least.

A copy of *The Budget* lay on the kitchen table, and Mose opened it up to the page where his column was.

"I read it, you know," she said.

Mose looked up, not surprised exactly, but perhaps bashful.

"You have a bright mind," she said. "You're able to simplify the *Ordnung*, show the reasoning behind the rules, give your thoughts... We all love that column."

"Even you?" he asked. And this time the words were fluent.

"*Yah*, even me." She smiled uncertainly. "Why, because I'm so liberal?"

He shrugged. "Aren't...you?"

"I've been told I am," she replied. "I don't think I am, though. I believe in our way of life. I love our culture, and our faith. I just think we should do more."

"More?"

"More for our neighbors," she said. "Isn't that the Christian way? We're supposed to love our neighbors, and do good for them."

"We do," he replied.

"We love our neighbors, and we keep them at arm's

length," she replied. "We make sure that we let them know that they are different. We speak another language around them. We dress differently—and don't get me wrong, I'm not saying we should relax our ideals at all! But if you were an *Englisher* looking in at us...would you feel welcome?"

Mose let out a slow breath. "We are different."

"Of course we are. But we use those differences as a fence. And that's the problem."

"We...we...have to protect our ways," Mose said.

"To the exclusion of others?"

"It's what keeps us unique and different." His stutter was still present, but he pushed past it in his attempt to speak. "If we wanted to be like the *Englishers*, we could all just become Mennonite."

"Ha ha, very funny," Naomi said with a rueful smile. "But don't the preachers say we are called to spread *Gott*'s love, as well as to protect our way of life? Who exactly are we spreading His love to?"

"To each other," he said.

"What about nonbelievers?" she pressed. "We sell them our wares, we feed them our pies, and they are perfectly happy to move on. They are intrigued by our buggies and horses, and... I don't even know what else."

"Laundry," he said.

"What?"

"Laundry—" He pointed to the window. "On the... line."

"Oh." She wrinkled up her nose. "Huh. Okay, so they're interested in those things, but that isn't what makes us so special. It's *Gott* in our lives. But what have they learned about *Gott*? Nothing."

"*Gott* works in...mys-mys—" Mose leaned back and didn't finish.

"*Yah*, He works in mysterious ways," Naomi agreed, not to be diverted from her argument. "But are we doing our part? We close ourselves off to protect ourselves from being influenced. I understand that. But what about our influence on others?"

Mose's eyes flickered with new interest, and again, he stuttered, but his words kept coming. "They are drawn to us, though. They come to see us. They come to see how we live, and how we raise our children."

"*Yah!*" she agreed. "They come, but we live behind the fence. And while we let them take a look, we don't let them participate."

"In what?" he frowned.

"In living, Mose!" She threw her hands up. "If they want to be like us, they'd have to learn our language, learn our way of life. They'd have to learn to farm, care for livestock... Standing on their side of the fence and watching us go about our lives, what good does that do any of them? What is most important about our Amish ways besides our faith in *Gott*?"

"Community," he said. "But...but..."

"*Yah—*" She didn't wait for him to finish this time and she plowed ahead. "But they aren't part of our community! Not really! And how can they be? We don't welcome them in. We keep them at a distance!"

Mose's eyes flashed, and he didn't answer her. Had she convinced him? Was he swayed by the strength of her argument? He pressed his lips together and rubbed his palms down his thighs. He wasn't convinced... She felt a wriggle of guilt.

"But you were going to say something, before I interrupted you," she said.

"N-n-nothing," he said.

"It was something," she said.

"You've...m-m—" He had to shut his eyes this time to get his control back. "...made up your m-m-mind."

This hadn't been her plan—to just bowl over him like that. She'd meant to let him say his piece, to even goad him into saying his piece! And now she felt a flood of regret.

"I'm sorry," she said. "I didn't mean to do that."

He just shook his head, his expression softening.

"No, really, Mose," she said. "Do you know what me being completely convinced I'm right gets me? Absolutely nothing. Because no one else agrees."

And it very likely kept her single, too. It wasn't her place to be full of opinions and want to change things. Amish communities didn't change—that was their unique strength, and if any inching forward happened, it came with the elders and the bishop having long discussions. It didn't start with one person's opinion.

"If a man stands on a table," Mose said slowly, stuttering over some words, but pushing forward all the same. "And if you grab his hand, are you more likely to pull him down, or for him to pull you up?"

"To pull him down," she said, and she sighed. "I do understand that the *Englishers* would likely change us, too. I know that it's easier to be pulled down than to improve someone else. I know we have to protect our ways, or we'll lose everything that we hold dear. I just..." She batted a loose curl out of her eyes. "Does your heart ever pull you somewhere, Mose?"

Mose's lips turned up in a slow smile, and his dark gaze caught hers. There was something about that direct look, strong, confident, and her heart skipped a beat. But before he could answer, she heard Claire and Aaron on the stairs.

They both looked over as Claire came down, Aaron in tow. The boy's face was rosy from being washed.

"Let me get the roast out of the oven," Naomi said, and she headed for the big, black stove. She used the oven mitts to open the door, and then pulled out the roasting pan.

"That looks perfect," Claire said as she came up behind Naomi. "Let me get the gravy into a bowl."

"Thank you, Claire." Naomi cast her friend a weak smile.

"Everything okay?" Claire asked softly.

"I'm scandalously liberal, Claire," Naomi said softly.

Claire rolled her eyes. "You aren't really."

But tell that to the men. For all of her talking, sometimes Naomi found it easier to express herself with a gesture, like cooking. Words could tangle her up and get in her way, but a good meal filled bellies and hearts at the same time. She didn't really expect Mose to understand where she was coming from, because no one else did, either. And the more she tried to explain herself, the worse she looked.

Mose was misunderstood because he couldn't get his ideas out. She was misunderstood no matter how much she tried to explain herself.

Mose didn't talk much through the meal, but the food was so good that no one did until plates were polished. The lamb was tender and spiced to perfection. The mashed potatoes and gravy were the best he'd ever had, and he made a point of dishing himself up a heaping serving of salad, which, to his surprise, was incredibly tasty because she'd added an oil and vinegar dressing as well as some crumbled goat cheese and candied walnuts. That was a whole lot fancier than Amish women normally cooked, but he had to admit that it was delicious. When the meal was over, he accepted a plate of molasses and oatmeal pie, a comfortingly simple Amish dish.

When they were finished eating, Naomi gathered the plates and brought them to the sink, and Claire headed toward the side door.

"I'll get started on chores outside, Naomi," Claire said.

"Out-outside?" It was the first time Mose had uttered a word since the beginning of the meal, but it suddenly occurred to him that these two women were doing everything—the men's chores as well as the women's. And here he was an able-bodied man with a belly full of good food, and he wasn't going to let a woman go do a man's work while he was present.

Claire froze in surprise, and the two women exchanged a look.

"I'll...I'll do...it." He rose from his chair, wishing that the words were coming out of his mouth more easily, but there wasn't much to say. There was a stable out there, horses, and all the regular chores that he'd been a part of since he was Aaron's size. The little boy looked up at Mose with an expression of surprise, too.

There was no man in this house to show the little fellow what men did.

"Th-th-there's men's work," he said to the boy. "And th-th-there's work for w-w-women." It was more than he wanted to say in front of anyone, and he hated the sound of the stuttering, but he felt that there was something to be taught here, and the boy needed to understand what a man's job was around here. He pointed out the window. "We men…work…out there."

Mose had more to say than that—like how if a man could make things easier for a woman, he should do that, and how a man used his body to keep a home running, and there was pride in that—but he'd already stumbled over his words enough, and he didn't have the strength to keep going. So he turned and headed for the door.

The women didn't say anything as he put his hat back on and stepped out into the evening cool. A blue jay chattered at him from high in a tree, and he headed across the gravel and grass toward the wooden stable beyond. He didn't turn back to look at the house until he arrived at the stable. Then he allowed himself one glance over his shoulder and spotted Naomi in the window. Her fingers fluttered in a wave, and he waved back, feeling a little self-conscious, then walked into the stable. The door bounced shut behind him.

For a moment he just stood there. He felt more comfortable in a stable than he did trying to avoid polite conversation in a kitchen, and the solitude wrapped around him like a comforting blanket.

Gott, *I feel like a fool*, he prayed.

He couldn't get words out, and everyone could out-talk him, or talk over him. Naomi, too. Somehow, it made it worse that she was actively trying not to, because she had an advantage over him. A woman had to hold herself back in order to not trample him in a conversation. It shouldn't be that way, but it always had been.

But give him a pen and paper, and there was no stutter. There was nothing holding the words back when he wrote. And there was no talking necessary when he worked, either…unless you counted driving that wagon, in which case the *Englishers* loved nothing more than trying to engage him in conversation.

He scanned the stable, spotted the wheelbarrow leaning against a wall and grabbed it along with a shovel. The stalls needed mucking out, and he spotted a few rails that were getting loose, as well as a feed trough that needed to be fixed, as it had been replaced with a plastic bucket. This was a stable that hadn't had a man's hand in it for some time, and there was something about that that sparked some sympathy inside of him.

He worked for a good half hour mucking out three stalls when the door opened and Naomi stepped inside.

"Thank you for doing this, Mose," she said.

He nodded. *"Yah."*

"Claire is going to finish up in the kitchen," she went on. "I thought I'd come out and give you a hand."

"It's…okay," he said. He could do this much.

"Maybe I could give you some company?" She smiled hesitantly.

What could he say to that? *"Yah."* He returned her smile. "That would be nice."

Funny—she used to be his company back when they

were kids, too. He was the youngest of eight children in his family, and his next oldest brother was five years older. His parents had referred to him as their "surprise blessing." He didn't have playmates among his siblings, but he had had Naomi.

"It's harder with other people around, isn't it?" she asked.

"*Yah...*" He sucked in a breath. "I get...nervous."

"Are you nervous with me?" She met his gaze, and he saw uncertainty there. Of course, he was nervous with her! She was beautiful, smart, talkative... And she'd had his heart since he was ten.

"Nah," he said with a shrug, and he felt a rush of pride at the smile that broke over her face.

"Good," she said. "It's really something to see you again, Mose. I didn't hear about you, and I thought you'd be married by now. I was kind of afraid to ask your uncle how you were, you know? It would seem like I was fishing, and..." She didn't finish the thought.

It was the man's job to come courting, not a woman's job to put out feelers for him. But he'd never imagined that she'd given him another thought.

"You could have fished." The words came out with only a couple of halts.

Color touched her cheeks. "I do have some pride, Mose."

"I don't." He shot her a grin. "That meal was in-in-incredible."

"Oh, thanks." She blushed, lifted her shoulders. "I did put in some effort tonight."

"*Yah*? F-for me?"

"*Yah*, for you." She dropped her gaze. "Maybe I wanted to show off a little."

"I was impressed," he said.

"Good. I'd hoped you would be." She met his gaze with a teasing look of her own.

There was an open bale of hay on the other side of the stable, and he wheeled the barrow over to fill it. Naomi stayed where she was, leaning against the rails of a stall.

"You n-need help," he said. "With the m-men's work."

Naomi sighed. "*Yah*. I do. I've been talking to my sister about hiring someone to give us a hand with the outdoor chores. Claire and I are getting much busier with more tourist groups coming by, more bed-and-breakfast guests, and now with Claire's basket weaving classes, we're run off our feet just keeping the house guest-ready."

"Just hire someone," he said. And this time he wasn't even noticing his own stutter. He met her gaze.

"It's also a matter of finding someone," she said. "The boys in our immediate area have to work on their family farms. Actual ranch hands want full-time work, not just a bit here and there from people like us. It's harder than you think."

He nodded. "I…I can help. While I'm here."

"Would you?" She shook her head. "Mose, I'm supposed to be helping you, not the other way around."

"I…talk better when I'm b-busy," he said.

Her expression changed, and she nodded. "I did notice that. You aren't stuttering as much out here. I thought it was just having Claire around—"

And it was, a little bit. But keeping his hands busy

helped his brain to relax a bit more, and focus less on bungling up his words.

"All right," she said after a moment. "As long as we do the work together. Because I feel lazy just standing around like this."

Mose wheeled the barrow back to the first stall and Naomi picked up the pitchfork and began to spread the hay over the newly cleaned cement floor. A curl fell down her cheek and she didn't seem to notice. All of his attention was on that curl, because it shone like rose gold in the sun, and he couldn't help but wonder what it would feel like between his fingers.

Naomi straightened, and she seemed to feel his gaze on her, because she noticed the tendril then and secured it back under her *kapp*.

"Sorry," she said with a faint smile. "My hair is always flying out of my bun."

"It's...pretty." That wasn't quite what he'd meant to say. He'd wanted to say it was okay, he didn't mind, he wasn't offended...something like that. But a deeper truth had fallen from his lips instead.

"Oh..." Naomi smiled. "Thank you. I used to hate my hair, you know. It was nothing like the other girls'. Theirs was smooth and perfect, and mine is more true to my personality—an explosion." She laughed at her own joke.

"I like it," he said, then he paused. "I'm...sorry about Klaus."

"It's okay—"

"No!" This time he cut her off. "It's...it's not. It's... rude and...wrong. Klaus is...a fool."

"I'm not easy to match, and I know it," she replied.

"My sister is a matchmaker and even she had trouble with me. That should tell you something. Maybe it's why I want to drag some *Englishers* into our midst."

His stomach dropped, and he shot her a look of surprise.

"T-to marry?" he asked.

"No!" Naomi rolled her eyes. "But next to a bunch of *Englishers*, I'm downright safe, you know?"

"Yah." He wasn't so fortunate, though. Standing him next to *Englishers* wouldn't fix what made him different.

"I'm joking, of course. But I do give that impression, don't I?" Naomi asked with a sigh.

"What?" he asked.

"Of being a rebellious woman, of wanting to jump the fence," she said. "I don't think I'm actually so different from the other women—I just don't hide things as well! They're better at keeping their thoughts to themselves, and mine come out of my mouth before I think better of them. At my age, I'm not sure I'll improve, either."

"That's…a blessing," he said. At least she was honest. The Bible had a lot to say about people who pretended to be better than they were.

Naomi put the pitchfork down with a clank of metal against concrete floor. "We're polar opposites, you and me, Mose. I talk too fast, and you aren't able to say everything in your head."

Mose met her gaze. "It's h-hard being d-d-different."

"Amen to that," she murmured, then she smiled. "But a good friend helps."

Yah, a good friend did help. With Naomi and her wild

hair and even wilder way of thinking, he didn't feel so alone—she'd always had that effect on him.

But she was right—Naomi was an example of why the *Ordnung* was so important. Everyone needed to be reined in, given boundaries, made to pause and think. Because if everyone just swung off after their own inclinations, there wouldn't be any Amish community anymore. Everything they valued—the togetherness, the simplicity, the traditions—would be nothing but a memory.

But looking at Naomi, catching her glittering green eyes, he couldn't be the one to hold her back. He could try, but in the end, he wouldn't be able to do it because she'd always been his weakness. Add to that, she could out-argue him because of his stutter alone. And whoever married Naomi would have to hold her back from a lot of her wild ideas, or follow her straight to perdition.

Mose felt his face heat and he wheeled the barrow off toward the door to dump it. She was helping him get more comfortable with talking. That was all. And he'd best remember it.

Chapter Four

That evening, after Aaron was sound asleep in his little bed next to his mother's in their upstairs bedroom, Naomi sat at the kitchen table with a hot cup of tea in front of her. The evening was far too warm for tea, but she'd made it anyway because mint tea had always comforted her, ever since she was a little girl. And there had been many a disappointment that had needed the nursing of a hot, sweet cup of mint tea.

"Are you okay?" Claire asked, coming back down the stairs again. She had a towel wrapped around her head, having just washed her long dark hair.

"I'm fine," Naomi said.

"You like him, don't you?" Claire asked.

"Mose?" There was no use pretending she didn't know whom Claire meant. "He was a good friend many years ago. I'm glad to see him doing well."

"He's looking for a wife," Claire said. "And you're looking for a husband."

"Not anymore," Naomi replied.

"Why not?" Claire sat down opposite her and took

her hair down. She had a comb and she started to work out the tangles.

"You know, when Jacob Knussli came back to town, he was looking for a wife," Naomi said.

"He married your sister, though," Claire replied.

"*Yah, yah,* and I'm not pining for him, trust me," Naomi said. "But I saw my sister fall in love and find the man who was perfect for her all because a man was in want of a wife. I thought then that maybe it could work for me—Adel could arrange something and I'd have my loving husband, too. But it's a lot more complicated than that."

"Klaus." Claire's lips turned down at the mention of his name.

"He was perfect on paper," Naomi said, tapping the table. "He was a farmer who wanted a wife. He was known to be a hard worker and honest. He had an impeccable reputation. You know how it was—that arrangement was almost done before he'd even met me! And then…he met me."

"You still don't know why he ran like that?" Claire asked.

"No idea. We had one buggy ride, and he dropped me off at home and never came back." Naomi couldn't help the way her voice shook and she turned her attention back to the tea.

"Maybe he wasn't so ready for marriage to a stronger woman," Claire said. "Maria Friesen is very quiet. I met her a few times over the years at various gatherings. She's timid, shy, and I don't think she'd voiced an opinion in her life. He wanted a meek woman, and he found one."

"That's the thing." Naomi sipped her tea and put the teacup back down on the saucer. "Arranged marriages are a delicate balance. Both people need to be sure that their partner will live up to their hopes. Klaus was hoping for someone very different from me. Arranged marriages involve a lot more negotiation than I want to go through. I thought I could do it, but I'm glad I experienced Klaus, because at least I know now that I'm a little too softhearted to manage it. I'll have to meet a man the old-fashioned way."

"At a singing?" Claire asked.

"Maybe." Naomi smiled faintly. "I've started to pray a new prayer, Claire. I'm now asking *Gott* to throw the right man in my path, or fling me into his. I don't care anymore, but I'm done putting myself out there like a horse at auction. I'm a woman, not a Thoroughbred."

"It sounds a little rough, all that throwing and flinging—people are bound to get bruised," Claire said with a low laugh.

"As long as *Gott* is the one who handles me, I'm happy," she replied. "I'm safe in His hands."

"And you don't think that Mose coming along might be an underhanded toss from *Gott*?" Claire asked with a twinkle.

"Mose is looking for an arranged marriage," Naomi said. "I can't do that. I can't just walk into an arrangement and hope he doesn't regret it later...or hope that he lights up when I come into the room a year from now...ten years from now. I won't do an arrangement. My heart can't take it. Did you know Leah and Daniel Lantz?"

Claire shook her head.

"Theirs was an arranged marriage," Naomi replied. "Leah's from Redemption, and she was a Good Apple, like me. Single and a little older… You know what they say—we're too high up the tree to pick easily. More likely, we're just too high up in age. Well, a well-respected man from Ohio wanted a wife, and he came looking in Redemption. We didn't have a matchmaker then, but had some resourceful older women who put their heads together and arranged the marriage. Apparently, Leah and Daniel seemed like an excellent match. Leah was pretty and a good cook. She was bright and cheery. Daniel was very serious and reliable. What could possibly go wrong?"

"What did go wrong?" Claire asked with a grimace.

"They couldn't get along. He wanted her to stop being so cheery and to be more sober and serious. She was just too liberal for him. He couldn't take it. They fought and fought, and there were no children from the marriage. Eventually, he moved to Ohio to clear his head. That was two years ago."

"He never came back?" Claire gasped.

"He just left." Naomi turned her cup on the saucer. "I have plenty of good reason not to want an arranged marriage, and it isn't just because of Klaus. I'm too much like Leah, and Mose is too much like Daniel. I'm not so cocky as to think the same things can't happen to us."

"You don't think arranged marriages work?" Claire asked softly.

"I think they can…" Naomi shot her friend a sympathetic look. "Are you thinking of putting your pie on the table, so to speak?"

"No, no," Claire replied. "It's the same thing I told

your sister when she was looking for a wife for Jake—I have a son to consider, and marriage is for life. I can't marry a man that quickly and just take the chance on him loving my son the way Aaron deserves to be loved by his stepfather. It's not just my heart at stake—it's Aaron's."

"Well, I wish Mose many blessings on his search for a wife," Naomi said. "And I'll do my best to help him with his stutter so that he can find a good woman."

Claire nodded. "Do you know what we'll serve the congresswoman when she comes for lunch tomorrow?"

Naomi blinked. She'd forgotten about Congresswoman Gates's visit in the excitement of seeing Mose Klassen again. It had been arranged weeks ago, and for the *Englishers* this would be a very high honor indeed. But they were Amish, and while they appreciated the hard work that public servants did, they didn't put them on the same kind of pedestal.

"I wonder why she's coming," Naomi said.

"A photo op?" Claire said with a shrug.

"With a horse, perhaps," Naomi chuckled. "It won't be a picture with us."

"Of course…" Claire smiled faintly. "But it does make me a little nervous. I don't like a lot of extra attention, especially not from politicians and the press."

"Well, let's just serve the lunch we normally serve tourists," Naomi said. "A congresswoman is a person, too, and she'll love our soup and bread as much as everyone else does."

When people of position visited the Amish, they got the unique experience of being just likc everyone else. That was part of the Amish belief system. No one was above another. Everyone was equally humbled before *Gott*—even politicians.

Besides, maybe having a visit from Congresswoman Gates would help distract Naomi from thinking about Mose more than she should. He was a conservative Amish man in search of an arranged marriage. He wouldn't be looking in her direction for that.

This time around, she wouldn't be making a fool of herself.

The next day, the congresswoman arrived in a sleek, black car. She came alone—no photographers, no staff members—and she got out of her vehicle dressed in a dark blue skirt suit with matching blue pumps. Her graying hair was done in a chin-length bob, and when she pushed a button on a fob, the car blinked and gave a chirp.

Locked.

Aaron stood in his little broadfall pants, a proud smile on his face as he waited to meet the congress-woman...or rather, he waited for the congresswoman to tell him what a handsome little fellow he was, and she didn't disappoint.

"Well, hello, young man," she said with a smile. She held out her hand and Aaron shook it with two exaggerated pumps.

"Hello," he said.

"Don't you look handsome," she said.

Aaron beamed, and Naomi laughed. "Welcome. My name is Naomi, and this is Claire. This little guy is Aaron."

"My name is Eleanor." She smiled easily. "I know

you do first names here, and can I just tell you what a relief it is to drop all the formality."

"Oh, really?" Naomi hadn't expected that. "Well, it is our way."

"The Amish bring a lot of good, solid integrity to our great state," Eleanor said, following Naomi inside. Claire and Aaron took up the rear and once she came inside, she shot Aaron another smile. "We can all learn a little bit from how you live."

Naomi went to the stove, where a pot of homemade tomato soup was keeping warm, and Claire went to the icebox for the fresh butter from Petersheim Creamery that they'd serve with crusty rolls.

"We just do what we believe is right," Naomi said, bringing the filled soup tureen to the table.

"Even when it's hard," Eleanor said, taking a seat. "You follow your conscience, even when it would be so much easier not to."

"The right path is normally the narrow one," Claire agreed.

They bowed their heads in silent prayer, and Naomi noticed that Eleanor did, too—without the usual discomfort that came from guests not used to their ways. When they raised their heads, Naomi served her some soup, and Eleanor waited until everyone else had their bowls filled, too, before she dipped her spoon into the soup and took a mouthful.

"Delicious," she murmured. "I grew up on Campbell's canned soup, and this reminds me of that."

"Naomi is a terrific cook," Claire said, casting Naomi a smile. "I've tried to follow her recipes, and nothing comes out just the way she does it."

"I don't know why," Naomi replied. "But it's my gift, I suppose. I cook. It's what I do."

For the next few minutes it was general chitchat while they all ate their fill, and when Eleanor pushed her bowl back with a smile, she said, "That was delicious. Thank you so much. Now... I was hoping to discuss something with you ladies."

"Oh?" Naomi frowned.

"It's an idea I have for our communities helping each other," Eleanor went on.

"Oh, you can stop there," Naomi said, shaking her head. "We're women. We don't make those decisions. You'd need to talk to the bishop and elders. They're the ones who decide...well, anything."

"I wanted the opinion of a woman first," Eleanor said. "Besides, I feel like I can connect better with hardworking businesswomen like yourself. Too many times a man will simply shut down when it comes from a woman he doesn't know. And I've heard from a friend of mine who came to stay at your bed-and-breakfast that you're open-minded and you care about others."

It was nice to know their reputation had preceded them.

"Well...we could give our opinions, at least, couldn't we?" Naomi cast a questioning look at Claire.

"I think we could," Claire agreed.

Aaron was squirming in his seat, so Claire sent him outside to play, and the boy scampered off.

"I've long admired the Amish work ethic," Eleanor said. "I was raised by a single mother, so I know what it means to work hard. I saw my mother work two and three jobs just to keep the bills paid, and she made sure

I had three square meals every day. On her own, that was no easy feat. I often credit my mother's hard work for how I turned out. I learned right and wrong, and how to put some serious effort into my jobs from her."

Claire smiled wistfully, and Naomi nodded. "Hard work is important, especially for little ones to learn from their parents."

"We have a lot of young people who don't have the benefit of that kind of example," Eleanor went on. "In government, we call them at-risk youth. Basically, that just means that these are young people who have everything against them, and chances are, they'll make bad choices."

"Hmm." Naomi wasn't sure what the congress-woman was getting at.

"We've found that a job, a mentor and a wholesome environment can make all the difference for these kids, especially during the summers. And we'd like to propose a summer program that would link at-risk youth with an Amish job and mentor who'd give them some honest advice, and teach them a new skill during the summer months when they're off school."

"Oh!" Naomi smiled. "That is an interesting idea."

"Do you think?" Eleanor asked, and there was hope in her eyes.

"One thing to keep in mind," Claire added, "is that our faith is a big part of who we are. If we were talking to young people, we'd be talking about *Gott* in our lives, too. There's no way of getting around it."

"What these kids need are solid values and personal connection," Eleanor said, leaning her elbows on the table. "And personal connection is just that—personal!

Faith is a part of people's lives, and I think these kids could benefit from it."

"You're a Christian?" Naomi asked.

"I am." Eleanor nodded. "I was raised going to church."

"I've been wanting to find ways for our community to reach out to you *Englishers*," Naomi said, and she paused, grimacing. "I know how that sounds. Us. You. Such a divide between us. But I don't think there should be. We have our ways that we protect, but we're all people, and we're all *Gott*'s children. Personally, I'd love to have a young person around here."

She looked over at Claire, but Claire's expression was more guarded. Did she not find this exciting? Eleanor was smiling now.

"I was hoping you'd feel that way," the congress-woman said earnestly. "I know it might take some thought and time for others to come to the same conclusion, but we all help each other, don't we? You benefit from police protection, even our military's work in protecting American soil. At heart, we're all Americans. And I think it would be wonderful if we could work together. Your faith and your way of life is a unique addition to the American scrap quilt, if I can use that imagery. And I'd love to work together with you."

"What sorts of things would we do with the…at-risk youngsters?" Naomi asked.

"Well, give them jobs to start with," Eleanor said. "They need to learn how to work for what they make. We'd have to have some rules, of course. There would be some jobs reserved for the youth, and there would be some government subsidization to help create work for them… But what sorts of jobs would really be decided with your community. What sorts of jobs do you think would benefit a teenager?"

"Working with animals," Naomi said. "Learning some basic farm work is good for character. But there are other jobs, too. Cleaning up after craftsmen is one that jumps to mind. Or working in the garden. Or selling produce at a roadside stand…"

"Excellent ideas," Eleanor said. "Do you have any concerns about this idea? Challenges we should be thinking about?"

Yes, Naomi was sure that there would be plenty—and somehow she wasn't thinking about the bishop's worries right now. She was wondering what Mose would say about this. Would he see the positive? Or would he see the risk? The risk—she knew it. And yet, she still wanted to hear what he thought on the issue because he explained himself well. At least in his column he did.

Naomi looked over at Claire.

"*Yah*, a few," Claire said. "What if the young people don't want to cooperate? Our young people have been working hard since they were Aaron's age. What if these young people just won't listen? We raise our young ones from birth to know how to mind their parents and respect their elders. These young ones wouldn't have been raised so well."

"But they wouldn't be beyond saving, either, Claire," Naomi said. "I know I'm not a mother myself, but these kids deserve a chance."

"These would be youths, teenagers," Claire said. "Not little ones. Am I right?"

"Yes, that's right," Eleanor said.

Naomi and Claire exchanged a look, then Naomi sighed. "There would be challenges, Eleanor, but your idea has merit. I believe that *Gott* is calling us to grow, to deepen. We won't change, but maybe He has something we can share with the outside world."

"Do you think I might be able to meet your bishop?" she asked.

"Of course, anyone can speak with him. He's just a local farmer," Naomi said, and she paused, her mind spinning over the idea that this congresswoman had provided. It was exciting, fresh, and would be immediately rejected. "But maybe you should let me bring it up to the bishop. You might have a better chance of him agreeing if he's had some time to think about it first."

"I would appreciate that very much," Eleanor agreed. "I want you to know that I won't pester your community, but I thought it was worth a shot, at least. Would you be willing to give me an address for the bishop?"

"Of course," Naomi replied with a smile. "I'm not someone who makes these decisions anyway, so you'll want to talk to him. I'll go talk to him tomorrow, and you can go see him anytime after that."

This was the sort of idea that Naomi had been yearning for—a way to connect two communities in a meaningful way. She'd wanted to share their faith in a way that would change lives, and what better way to do it than to encourage at-risk young people? Maybe *Gott*'s hand was in this. Maybe it would meet with success.

And yet, her mind kept going back to Mose. What would he say when she told him about it? And as if on cue, she heard the sound of hooves outside. The tourist buggy was here.

"We'd best clean up!" Claire said, standing quickly. "We have a tour group and pie sampling. I'm so sorry to rush you, Eleanor, but I'll need to set out the pies."

"Of course, of course!" The congresswoman rose to her feet. "And thank you for letting me bounce this idea off of you. I appreciate your time, ladies, and the delicious lunch."

Mose reined the big quarter horse in, and he looked curiously at the glossy black car sitting in the drive. It looked expensive, although he couldn't say exactly why, but if that was a buggy, it would be top-of-the-line. The door of the bed-and-breakfast opened and an older *Englisher* woman came out. She was dressed in dark blue, which seemed to set off her silvering hair rather nicely, he had to admit. She looked slim, fit and equally expensive as that car.

Again, he wasn't exactly sure why.

"Congresswoman Gates!" someone in the back of the buggy exclaimed, and there was a sudden flurry of excitement as the rest turned to see.

The woman looked up, a smile spread over her face, and waved. She was wearing makeup—something Amish women didn't do. It made her eyes stand out more, her lips pinker, and her skin look smoother than it should naturally. He'd never liked that perfecting look of makeup. He preferred the naturally bright eyes and easily blushing cheeks of women like Naomi. Her hair was never perfect—always exploding out of her *kapp*—but it was perfectly lovely.

He had to stop this… Naomi wasn't the right woman for him, no matter how pretty she was, or how much she seemed to dominate his thoughts. A decision to buy a buggy was an important one. A buggy might last him fifteen years. A decision to buy a piece of property was also important—land could be the beginning of financial stability, but it could be sold if he changed his mind. But a wife? A wife was a choice for a lifetime—there was no changing his mind—a wife had to be trusted with his heart, his home and his happiness for the rest of his days. It had to be a logical decision.

"Hello!" the congresswoman called. "It's a beautiful day!"

Mose watched as several of his passengers hopped down. They pulled out their cell phones and started taking pictures. The woman came to talk to them, and smiled brightly as they took pictures with her, their phones held out at arm's length.

A politician. The *Englishers* sure dealt with leadership differently than the Amish did. The bishop was respected, but he was also chosen by lot, not by election. *Gott* chose their leaders, and they never turned the bishop, elders or deacons into anything more than what they were—servants of the community to be respected and obeyed, but not to be worshipped in any way.

The door opened again, and this time Naomi came out and bent down to put a rock in front of the screen to hold it open. Her clear green gaze moved over the excited guests, and then landed on him. A smile touched her lips.

Mose hopped down from the wagon seat and he gave an older gentleman a hand down. He seemed to be taking the tour with his adult daughter, and Mose helped her down as well. That left the wagon empty. He looked up to see Naomi coming in his direction, and he felt a wave of relief. He'd been avoiding conversation for hours now, and with Naomi, he didn't need to. It was a strange luxury.

"Who...who...who—" He didn't finish, but jutted his chin toward the congresswoman who was moving toward her car now.

"That's Eleanor Gates, our congresswoman," Naomi replied. "She booked a private lunch with us, and it turned out that she wanted to talk to us, specifically. She had some ideas. Rather good ideas, I have to admit."

Mose's heart sank. Little good came from *Englisher* ideas. "Oh?"

The congresswoman broke free from the excited people and came in their direction. She smiled at Mose and held out a hand to shake.

"I'm Eleanor," she said.

"Mose," he said, and he shook her hand.

"Pleasure to meet you, Mose," she said, then turned to Naomi and held out a hand to her, too. "It was nice to talk with you today, Naomi. Let's stay in touch, yes?"

"*Yah*. Definitely," Naomi replied.

The woman turned back toward her vehicle and got inside, then she pulled slowly out of the drive as Claire ushered the people into the house, little Aaron standing proudly next to her while the women exclaimed and gushed over how cute he was. Mose couldn't really blame them—Aaron was a cute kid. When the screen door clattered shut behind them, he exhaled a pent-up breath.

"What...what...what...idea?" he asked.

"A way to bring some at-risk youth to our community and show them a better way to live," Naomi said. "She'd like to work with the Amish community to show them how to work hard, and to gain some wisdom from our way of life."

She talked for a little bit about different jobs that might be offered to the young people, and how they weren't raised to understand the values the Amish held most dear. He could see that the idea was an exciting one to Naomi, but he could also see something she didn't.

"And what…what…what—" He shut his eyes. "What do we get?"

"Us?" Naomi blinked at him. "Nothing. I mean, there would be some financial support to make sure the young people are paid for work we otherwise wouldn't hire them to do, but… What do you mean, Mose?"

"You t-t-t-talk about what…what…" He was tempted to give up, but Naomi's gaze was locked on his face, no sign of impatience, so he plunged on, his words halting. "You talk about what we can do for them. But they are only taking. What about our young people? What about the damage this might do to them?"

"They would see what happens when *kinner* go down the wrong path, I imagine," Naomi said.

That wasn't quite his own experience with teenagers. They were drawn to the rebellious and the dangerous because it seemed most exciting. He just shook his head.

"What about the story of the Good Samaritan?" she asked. "Should we be like the church rulers who went to the other side of the street when someone was in need of help?"

"No," he said. "Of c-c-course not. I care about their

children, but f-f-forgive me, I care m-m-more about ours!"

"Maybe it isn't about their young people or ours," Naomi said. "Maybe it's just about teenagers who need guidance. They need what we have, Mose." Naomi looked up at him pleadingly, and he had a hundred arguments for why this was a bad idea, but there was something in her eyes that stilled his tongue. She was an idealist, he realized then. She thought that everything would go well because of her pure intentions. And truly, her intentions were good—he knew that. But she was wrong, all the same.

Still, she was also so hopeful, so endearing, so full of energy. She was hard to resist. Let someone else talk her out of it. This wasn't his responsibility, and maybe he didn't want to be the one to ruin this for her.

"You should t-t-talk to the b-bishop," he said.

"Oh, I'm going to," Naomi said with a nod. "I told Eleanor that I'd bring it up to him first so that he can have some time to really think it over before she goes to see him herself. It gives the plan a better chance."

So she was going to be right in the middle of this *Englisher* plan to bring their damaged young people into their midst. This was like when they were children, and she'd dream up some extraordinary game and he'd just be caught up in her current and swept along with her. Her games were never bad, but they were often daring, and they all originated in her own imagination. She could almost get her make-believe stories to come true just by the sheer force of her will. But they weren't children anymore.

Mose had a lot more to say, but it was difficult to get

the words out. Maybe that was for the best. He'd heard other men pray that *Gott* would put a hand over their mouths sometimes, but he'd never had that problem. He lived his whole life with *Gott*'s hand over his mouth.

"Do you remember being seventeen?" Naomi said quietly, leaning against the wagon next to him. "The farm seemed too small and cramped, and the world seemed so exciting..."

"You had...had...had...an *Englisher* boyfriend," he said.

She looked over at him in surprise. "What? He wasn't a boyfriend. How did you hear about him?"

"My aunt."

She blushed a little. "Okay, if I have to be completely honest, I'd hoped he'd look at me like that, but he never did."

"Oh..." That wasn't quite what his aunt and uncle had suspected, and the thought of her hoping for something she didn't get made his heart ache just a little bit. "You had your f-f-freedom, though."

"Yah." She let out a slow sigh. "As a teen, you think the world is so exciting, and that home is so dull. I remember being lonely back then. I hated my figure, my weight, my hair... I hated everything that made me me, you know?" She looked up at him. "And what I really needed wasn't an *Englisher* boyfriend or to make bad choices, it was to belong, to be appreciated. I think about these at-risk teens, and I remember being a teen myself. Except I had something that kept my feet on the ground."

"Yah." He dropped his gaze.

"Did you ever feel that way?" she asked.

He nodded. "I hated my s-s-stutter. I hated that I c-c-couldn't t-talk well. I was lonely, t-too."

Naomi leaned against his arm, her soft shoulder pressing warmly against him. He wished he could slide an arm around her, but there were still people to see, and he knew he couldn't do that to her reputation. So he dropped his hand and curled his fingers over hers. She froze, and he knew then that he'd gone too far, but she didn't move her hand away, and so he didn't, either.

"There is nothing easy about being young," she said after a few beats of silence. "Young people are sensitive. They hate things in themselves that they can't change, whether it's a stutter or their hair, or the way their body carries weight. And without a loving community, I don't know how they do it."

She looked up at him then, and his heart skipped a beat as he met her earnest gaze.

"You're a good woman," he said softly, and this time the words came out smoothly.

"I just want to help, Mose," she said. "If we don't help, who will?"

She'd mentioned the Good Samaritan, and she was right in the spiritual application, of course. Helping others never came without risk, but was it right to risk an entire community? A lot of change had already crept into his home community. Cell phones were used for safety. Buggies had seat belts where they lived. Barns were now fully electric, although homes weren't. Changes came slowly but surely. And were they necessary? Many would argue that they were, but they'd gone generations without such strides forward. Were they still protecting their distinctiveness as much as they should?

But something else had caught in his mind—she hadn't liked herself. She hadn't appreciated what a beauty she was, and that was a sad thought.

"I l-l-like your hair," he said.

"What?" She blushed then. "Really?"

Mose regarded her—the naturalness of her face, her golden red lashes that were so long when he looked down at her like this. And her soft roundness—it was comforting, beautiful. To think she'd hated any part of herself as a teenager... Someone should have told her she was absolutely perfect the way she was.

"And the r-rest of you, too," he said haltingly. "You're p-p-pretty."

Naomi dropped her gaze, but the tips of her ears were pink now. What was he doing? He'd had to force those words out, and somehow he still hadn't been able to stop himself. It didn't matter what he thought of her looks!

"You're kind, Mose."

He didn't know how to answer that, so he didn't. He just gave her fingers a little squeeze, and he released her hand. He was going too far, and he didn't even know why.

"Maybe there's another girl who needs a grown woman like me to tell her that she'll be grateful for her hips one day," Naomi said, "and that some comment by a thoughtless boy was just stupidity coming out of his mouth, not truth."

"You want to be a *mamm*," he said, the realization

dawning on him suddenly. She was talking about all the wisdom a mother passed down now.

"But I have no children of my own," she said. "I have to love *someone*, Mose."

She had so much love to give, so much that it was overflowing past her own community to the outsiders. She just wanted to love someone who needed it. He felt a lump rise in his throat.

The side door opened then, and Claire came out first, holding the screen for the *Englishers* to pass outside again. They were laden down with jars of preserves and white cloth bags that likely held some other wares that the women were selling.

"Thank you so much for coming," Claire was saying, her voice surfing the breeze toward them. "Remember us at Draschel Bed and Breakfast when you're planning your next getaway. We book a few weeks ahead of time, but we'd be so happy to have you back again."

It was time to continue on. Naomi moved a step away from him. She was doing the right thing—keeping appearances pure—but he missed the softness of her shoulder against him.

"I'll see you," he said.

She nodded, and then he had to help the first tourist back up into the buggy. Had Klaus seen the woman in Naomi before he'd decided so firmly against her? Had rejecting her been difficult for Klaus at all? Because as wrong as she was for Mose, she was ever so tempting.

But he'd never be able to be the husband who kept her to the Amish ways. She melted his heart too much, and he'd go right along with her, even though his conscience screamed against it.

A choice of wife was a cautious one. His heart couldn't lead here. Because left to its own devices, his heart would lead him right after Naomi, and right over a cliff.

Chapter Five

All that evening, Naomi thought about the feeling of Mose's hand covering hers. And he'd said she was pretty...a silly thing to make her blush at this age, but it still did. He was probably just being kind—feeling bad about Klaus, or remembering their childhood friendship. Because she knew that he heartily disagreed with her liberal views. But he was still... Mose. Sweet, handsome, earnest Mose.

And may *Gott* help her, but she wasn't hoping that he'd find a wife. She should be. He deserved one, but he wouldn't be holding her hand again, if he did. He wouldn't be putting his effort into getting his ideas out with her—he'd be doing that with someone else.

Still, her hand tingled when she remembered the feeling of his warm fingers cupping hers, and thankfully Claire didn't notice that Naomi was quiet and distracted since they had some *Englisher* overnight guests arrive and they were occupied with hosting them.

The next morning, Naomi drove her buggy to the bishop's farm. Bishop Glick was a kind older man who ran a dairy as well as acted as religious leader to their area. He was also Claire's second cousin, which gave Naomi a friendlier relationship to him. All the same, it truly was a sacrificial position since a bishop wasn't paid for his post, and it was a lifelong responsibility. The bishop had come back inside after his first round of chores, and he listened thoughtfully to what Naomi had to say.

"If you empty your barn in the fall for everyone else, who will feed you in the winter?" the bishop said quietly. "If we give away too much, if we drop our fences and open our arms, who will protect our own children from the bad influences? We shelter our children, show them a better way. Naomi, I know your heart is in the right place, but how do you expect our children to keep to the Amish path and not slide off into perdition if we don't set a firm example now? We are protecting them from the very life those *Englisher* young people are living. My heart goes out to them—it does—but protecting our way of life must be a higher priority."

Then the bishop had said a prayer with her, shaken her hand and wished *Gott*'s blessings upon her. He asked her to say hello to Claire and little Aaron for him, then he sent her on her way.

Now, as Naomi flicked the reins, guiding her horse down the familiar road toward her sister's new home on the Knussli farm, frustration simmered inside of her. The bishop was quiet and reassuring, gentle and considerate, and completely unable to see her perspective. How were they supposed to love others when they wouldn't help them in their time of need?

But there, behind her frustration, was the memory

of Mose and the way he'd held her hand… She'd best stop thinking about that, because while Mose might appreciate her, he'd never really understand her, and it didn't matter if he could make her stomach flip, because that didn't last. Mutual respect and understanding did.

The trees were still green, just a yellow leaf here or there, a promise of fall to come. There was a fresh undercurrent to the northern breeze that cooled her arms, and she ran through the arguments she could have made to the bishop, if arguing with a bishop was in any way acceptable.

Of course, she wouldn't argue. She couldn't. The bishop had heard her request and very kindly denied it. Would her sister be willing to mention it to the bishop? He did respect Adel's point of view…

As she turned down the road that led to the Knussli farmhouse, the rolling landscape tumbled out beyond, and she could see in the distance some patches of yellowing trees and the snaking curve of a stream that watered the land. It was a beautiful area.

The red barn had a new roof, and half of the sides had been painted a fresh coat of red. Adel's husband, Jacob, must still be working on it, and Naomi knew he'd be hurrying to get it done before winter.

Another buggy was parked next to the house, so it looked like her sister had a guest already, but as Naomi reined in her horse, the front door opened and Leah Lantz came out. Her face looked blotchy, like she'd been crying, and she quickly wiped at her eyes when she saw Naomi. Adel stood in the doorway, her pregnant belly doming her blue cape dress out in front of her.

"Good morning, Leah," Naomi said, hopping down from the buggy seat. "Are you all right?"

"Yah, yah..." Leah nodded quickly. "I'm fine. But thank you."

Naomi caught her friend's arm as she tried to rush past, and Leah's eyes brimmed with tears.

"Leah!" she said.

"I'm fine!" Her voice shook, and she obviously didn't want to talk about it.

"Okay, I won't pry," Naomi said. "But the minute you feel up to it, I want you to come to see me. We'll eat pie and we'll talk, okay?"

Leah nodded. *"Yah,* I will."

Leah headed toward her buggy, still hitched up. Naomi didn't say anything else, but she did wave again as the other woman pulled her buggy around in a circle to head back up the drive. Poor Leah.

"She isn't okay at all," Naomi said to her sister as she met her at the door. "What happened?"

"I can't say..." Adel shook her head. "But it's nothing new."

"She misses Daniel," Naomi guessed. "Those two might be terribly matched, but Leah does love him."

"It's heartbreaking when this happens," Adel said, gesturing Naomi inside and then shutting the door behind her. "This job of matching up couples...it's not always about just finding two people who could get married. It's about who *should*."

"You weren't responsible for Leah and Daniel, though," Naomi said.

"No, I wasn't, thankfully," Adel replied. "But they are a warning to me."

The Lantzes were a warning to Naomi, too, for that matter. Leah and Naomi had a little too much in common in their liberal ways for Naomi not to take the walking warning to heart.

"Are you worried about matching up Mose?" Naomi asked.

"I'm not worried. I'm…taking it seriously," Adel replied. She led the way through the sitting room and into the bright kitchen. "I made cinnamon rolls. Would you like one?"

"*Yah*, please." Naomi joined her sister at the big, solid kitchen table. A pan of cinnamon buns was already waiting, and Adel dished up two sticky, sugary buns onto plates and handed one to Naomi.

"How is Mose doing?" Adel asked. "I mean… communication-wise. Is he finding it easier to talk with you?"

"A little bit," Naomi said. "Honestly, Adel, I think I'm just getting used to it. His stutter is still very strong, and I think he has trouble getting all his ideas out. Obviously, he's very smart. He writes beautifully, doesn't he?"

"*Yah*, he does," her sister agreed.

"He's relaxing more," Naomi said. "You know, it isn't about his stutter at all. It's about whether or not he's willing to push past it and keep trying to get his thoughts across."

"And perhaps about the patience of the listener," Adel said.

Naomi unwound her cinnamon bun and tore off her first bite. It was delicious, as her sister's baking always was. When she swallowed, she said, "He needs a woman who won't mind waiting on his ideas a little bit."

"A quiet woman," Adel said.

"Hmm. Maybe." It wasn't quite what Naomi meant. He needed a woman who valued his ideas enough to wait. Was being quiet really such a valued quality? Who was she fooling? It tended to be.

"I'd love to find a husband for Claire," Adel said.

Why did Naomi feel a stab at the idea of Adel coming up with a name, especially someone so close to her? Naomi remembered that feeling of Mose's hand over hers... Just being friendly, surely, but...

"And I think she'd do nicely for Mose," her sister went on, "except that she won't do an arranged marriage. She'll need to be courted properly so that she can learn to trust the man who will be her son's stepfather. And I understand that in a new way, now that I'll have a child of my own soon. A *mamm* worries." She put her hand on her rounded belly.

"*Yah*, she did remind me of that," Naomi replied. "Her first priority is Aaron. As it should be."

"She's a good *mamm*." Adel paused, frowned. "Maybe Lydia Speicher. I was considering her because she's quiet and sweet, and likes to spend time with her needlework. She might have the right temperament. And she doesn't have any children to complicate her decision. She was someone I'd thought of for Jake." Her cheeks turned pink.

"*Yah*, I know," Naomi said with a chuckle. "And then you married him, yourself."

"I have to find her a good husband," Adel said with a sigh. "I owe her that much."

Naomi took another bite. "She might work for him considering that he's conservative. I've been driving him a little nutty with my ideas." She forced a smile.

"I'm sure you have." Adel grinned. "I haven't given up on matching you yet, either."

"Yah, yah…" Naomi sighed. "I'm a little bit like Claire now. I couldn't attempt an arranged marriage again. I know why it's good for Mose, but…"

"I know," Adel replied. "I still feel terrible about Klaus. He came with excellent references, and he had such a good reputation. Matchmaking is supposed to be easier, isn't it? A reasonably intelligent woman can see who would make each other happy."

"But try to convince them of it." Naomi shot her sister a smile. "As for me, I'm more shocking than you think." Naomi was attempting to joke, but it didn't come out that way, and her sister met her gaze.

"You need the right man," Adel said simply. "Everyone agrees—you need to be cooking for your own family."

Easier said than done, though. Naomi had been waiting on the right man for a long time. It was time to change the subject.

"The congresswoman came by yesterday, and she wasn't just coming for a tourist experience," Naomi said.

She explained about the visit and about Eleanor Gates's idea. When she stopped speaking, Adel was frowning.

"You hate it," Naomi said.

"I don't hate it," Adel replied. "But I don't think

it takes into account all the complications that come with it."

Naomi sighed. "Mose thinks the same thing, and so does the bishop. You're in good company there. But Adel, I think we could do more. Everything good comes with some risk. If it's what *Gott* wants us to do, He'll protect us."

"But what does *Gott* want us to do?" Adel asked.

"Maybe the congresswoman's idea is too aggressive," Naomi said. "We could start smaller, though. What about my idea to have a sewing circle that includes a few *Englisher* women?"

"The bishop already said it was too dangerous," Adel said.

"But maybe, if compared with the congresswoman's idea, my idea might seem a little better!" Naomi sighed. "Adel, you have responsibilities, and your husband, and your baby on the way. But I don't have anything more than the bed-and-breakfast."

"That's not true. You have Claire and Aaron, and you'll always have me!" Adel said. "This child will need a loving aunt!"

"Yah, yah..." Naomi agreed. Life was about more than just marriage, but she felt the hole in her life, all the same.

And when she thought about Mose, about his warm hand covering hers, about his halting but sweet compliments, she wished more than anything that she could have the family of her own that she longed for.

But Leah and Daniel were still a warning. Leah had longed for a husband, too, and she'd gotten married. Was her current heartbreak worth it?

"Oh, I was going to ask you if we can afford to hire someone part-time to help out with the men's work. Claire and I are getting so busy with the guests that it's getting harder to keep up. Mose is helping out a bit, and I don't mind saying, it's been a relief."

"And Jake is so busy, too," Adel said. "*Yah*, you know what? I think it's time you did. But make sure it's an Amish boy—I'm not sure if I have to say that outright, but please don't wait on some plan to help out youth at risk with the *Englishers*. You need someone now, and our guests want an Amish experience. If they saw an Amish boy working outside, they'd love it."

"That makes sense," Naomi agreed. "And I don't know why you even worry about these things, Adel. Where would I find an *Englisher* boy, anyway? But thank you. I'll find someone as soon as I can."

Naomi stood up and went to the window. She could see Jake loping back toward the house, and Naomi wasn't in the mood to watch her happily married sister and brother-in-law chat and steal touches when they thought Naomi couldn't see. And with that thought came the memory of Mose's hand covering hers so powerfully that her breath caught.

"I'd best get back," Naomi said. "Your husband is on his way in for lunch. I see him coming."

"Are you all right, Naomi?" Adel asked softly.

"*Yah*, I'm fine," Naomi said, and she realized those were the exact words that Leah had used, too.

Some problems could be solved with hiring a local teen, but others needed to be sorted out privately. Being "fine" was the polite answer, but her heart was starting to get complicated. She'd best sort this out before she got herself hurt.

Mose's mind had been on Naomi all day as the horses pulled the wagon down the familiar roads with his chattering, happy tourists taking in the sights behind him. He'd been thinking about how pretty she was, and how funny and full of ideas. He was thinking about how reckless he'd been to hold her hand like that, too.

What had he been thinking? It had been a strange combination of protectiveness and a spillover from their friendship all those years ago. She'd always meant more to him than she ever knew, and having her there next to him, remembering how his own cousin had insulted her, the protective boy had come out in him. He'd wanted to hold her hand...and maybe punch Klaus in the nose.

That was reckless, too, because he was a full-grown Amish man, and his morals didn't allow for violence, even in defense of his friend's honor. He wasn't some aggressive *Englisher* solving his problems with his fists. He was called to higher behavior than that...and maybe even higher behavior than holding Naomi's hand. Because if he had to be completely honest, even though she inspired those protective instincts in him, she wasn't his to protect.

At the bed-and-breakfast, where they stopped for pie tasting, Naomi was especially busy because there was a woman with Down syndrome who'd taken a liking to her and stayed close while she worked. He watched how kind she was, how patient with the young woman's repeated questions. Was Mose just another person with more needs than most in her eyes? That thought had stabbed at him as he drove the tourists on again. How much of her kindness was coming from a place of sympathy?

Mose had wanted some time alone with her, he realized, but he hadn't gotten it, and he wondered if that made him a little needy, too. He wanted to make her life easier, not add to her workload. He'd make sure he went back tonight and worked on some chores for her.

When he'd dropped the tourists back off at the parking lot where their cars waited, he drove the wagon back to his uncle and aunt's home for dinner, but his heart wasn't any less tangled.

Aunt Linda had a wonderful spread waiting for him. It had been a delicious meal with brown buttered noodles, potato salad and fried chicken. Aunt Linda was a great cook, and Mose had eaten two platefuls.

"The bishop asked for you specifically when he came by earlier," Abram said as Linda took the plates off the table.

"Am I in t-t-trouble?" Mose asked. It wasn't every day a visitor to a community was called into a meeting with the local bishop, and his mind skipped back to how he'd held Naomi's hand. Had he offended her? Had he overstepped? That was a silly worry—she'd just tell him straight…wouldn't she?

"No, you're an expert on the *Ordnung*," Abram replied, "and they need your insight."

"Oh. *Yah*." He felt a rush of relief.

"So, tomorrow evening at the bishop's farm. Just go after dinner. About seven. The bishop will be glad to have you be part of a discussion. About what—I don't

know. I'm not told those things, but it's something par-
ticularly tricky, the bishop says."

"I'll be g-g-glad to h-h-h-help," Mose replied. He
glanced at his watch. It was time to get back to Naomi's
place and help with chores before either of the women
got to it first. He gave his aunt a grateful smile, and she
smiled back. She understood his silent thanks.

When Mose arrived at the bed-and-breakfast, he unhitched his horse and sent it out to pasture. The sun was
getting low, casting long golden rays over the land, and
stretching shadows. The breeze was warm this evening,
and he rolled up his sleeves as he headed to the stable.
He looked toward the house, and the side door opened.

"Hi, Mose!" Claire called.

He waved.

"Naomi is doing chores already," Claire said.

So he hadn't been quick enough. The stable door
opened and Naomi appeared, wearing a long black
apron, and a piece of straw stuck in her wild curls that
just wouldn't stay neatly under her *kapp*.

"There she is!" Claire said with a brilliant smile, and
then disappeared back into the house.

Mose smiled hesitantly at Naomi. "I…I…I…prom-
ised to h—" He pressed his lips together, his words all
tangled up again. "To…help…w-w-with chores."

"Thank you. It's nice of you, Mose."

What was it about this woman that her simple compliments sank so deep for him? She didn't mean anything by it, he was sure, but he was still warmed to think
she thought he was nice, all the same.

"Y-you were b-busy today," he said.

"Oh, I was!" She turned back to the stable and held the door for him. "It was one thing after another all day long. But I did manage to go see my sister."

Mose followed her inside and picked up a shovel from where it leaned against the wall. It didn't look like Naomi had gotten much done yet, which he was glad to see because he'd rather do it himself.

"Oh, *yah*?" he said, and went into the first stall where Naomi had gotten started.

"Jake is working a farm alone, so he works incredibly hard," Naomi said, wheeling the wheelbarrow closer. "And if Delia Swarey's teenage sons weren't so busy running her own flower farm, I'd be tempted to hire them on to help out here, but she's got so much to be done to keep her own business running that it seems unfair to ask."

He didn't answer, but he did put his back into shoveling out the stall. "D-did your s-s-sister agree to h-h-hire s-s-s—" The last word wouldn't come out, and he stopped.

"*Yah*, she did agree to it," Naomi replied, not seeming to even notice his difficulty. "So I'll see if I can find someone who can help out on a part-time basis. It's harder than you'd think, though. Teens are working with their parents, and most men don't need extra work. But I do believe that *Gott* will provide. He always does."

A woman of faith. He regarded her for a moment.

"What?" she said.

"N-n-nothing." He turned back to shoveling.

"Oh, come on, Mose," Naomi said. "What were you thinking just then?"

Mose paused again and looked at her over his shoulder. "Th-that I l-l-like your f-f-faith."

"Oh." She smiled then. "Thank you."

Mose shoveled the first heaping pile of soiled hay into the wheelbarrow, then turned to scoop up another.

"Have you seen my sister today?" she asked.

He shook his head. "No."

"She has someone she's considering for you," Naomi said.

Mose stopped working again and turned. "Really? That f-f-fast?"

"What? You think Redemption is lacking Good Apples?" she asked with a laugh, but he saw something flicker in her gaze when she said it. Was that sadness?

"Wh-who is it?" he asked.

"I won't give you a name until my sister has hammered things out on her end," Naomi said. "Adel would never forgive me for stepping on toes there, but the woman she's thinking of is very sweet. She's quiet. Kind. Very good with her hands. She could probably knit you a full suit."

Mose froze.

"That's a joke." Naomi laughed and shook her head. "Oh, Mose, you are so earnest. No one is going to knit you a suit. That's a promise."

Mose felt his face heat. He hadn't meant to be quite so serious. "D-d-does she kn-kn-know about m-m-my—" He sucked in a breath, tired from the exertion of the sentence.

"She will, of course," Naomi said, and she paused. "Mose, this stutter isn't your fault."

"I know." That came out fluently at least.

"And it's nothing to be ashamed of," she said.

"I know."

"Okay, then." She sighed.

"B-b-back up," he said.

Naomi blinked, then took a step out of the stall. He went back to working, cleaning out the last of the soiled hay. But as he worked, his mind was spinning. There was a woman to meet. This was why he was here, wasn't it? He wanted to meet someone he could marry and start a family with. But somehow, the thought of meeting this stranger made him feel mildly panicky.

"H-how will I t-t-t-talk to her?" he asked as he put the last of the hay into the barrow.

"Like you talk to me, Mose," Naomi said, and she picked up the handles and wheeled it away. She disappeared out a side door, and he waited for a moment, then headed out of the stall and opened the next door.

Naomi came back in, wheeling the barrow up to where he stood.

"She w-w-won't be you," he said.

"She'll be better than me," Naomi replied, and looking back into her green eyes, he wished that was even a remote possibility. No one woman could live up to Naomi, but that was what a woman said when she wasn't interested in the man for herself. She said her friend was a better choice. It was a way of being kind, but making the point.

He turned back to working again, his mind sorting through his situation. A man with a debilitating stutter shouldn't be so terribly picky, and he didn't want to be. Naomi wasn't really an option for him, anyway.

"Are you nervous, Mose?"

Mose looked back at her and found her gaze locked on him with such open honesty that his heart skipped a beat.

"Yah," he admitted.

"Well, don't be. You have a lot to offer a woman. Remember that."

He had his brain, his ability to write, and strong muscles to get the men's work done.

"Isn't that why you came?" Naomi pressed. "You came to find a wife, right?"

"Yah," he said and he smiled slightly. "H-h-hoping to."

"If *Gott* can bring me an employee, then *Gott* can bring you a wife, too," she said. "Just have some faith. You and I will have our needs met. Wait and see."

He nodded. *"Yah.* You're r-r-right."

"I tend to be," she said jokingly. "I didn't tell you. I went to see the bishop, and he sided with you completely."

"I w-wouldn't be so s-sure about that," he replied. His words were coming out smoother now as he worked.

"What? Why?" she asked.

He knocked the shovel on the side of the barrow with a clang to shake loose the soiled hay. "I've been a-a-asked to go to a m-m-meeting t-tomorrow night with the b-b-bishop."

"About what?" she asked, her voice dropping.

He shrugged.

"And asked in what capacity?" she pressed.

"An ex-ex-expert on the *Ordnung*," he said.

"Oh…" she breathed and she sucked in a deep breath, her eyes lighting up. "I wonder if Eleanor went to see the bishop already... Maybe she did! Maybe with some time to think it over, the bishop is willing to consider it. Maybe!"

She was getting her hopes up, and he shouldn't have done that. It could be about anything from farming to emergency cell phone use.

"I...I...I don't know," he said.

"It's very possible, though," she said. "Oh, Mose, we have so much here. If you ever saw the *Englisher* world, you'd know what I mean. We have family bonds that span generations. We take care of each other in ways the *Englishers* just don't. And our faith upholds us through anything. We have so much that it feels downright wrong not to share it."

Did it? Because there were a lot of things that were deep and abiding blessings that were meant to be treasured, not spread about. Like marriage, for example, which was never meant to be shared outside of the two people. Some blessings were diluted when they were spread too far.

Drink waters out of thine own cistern, and running waters out of thine own well... Let them be only thine own, and not strangers' with thee. Let thy fountain be blessed: and rejoice with the wife of thy youth.

Mose smiled, though, and he wouldn't say anything more on the subject. He wouldn't have to be the one to ruin this for her. Whatever the bishop and elders decided was up to them.

"Will you tell me about it—if you're allowed?" Naomi asked. "I mean, if it's about helping the *Englisher* youths."

"Yah." He nodded. "If I'm a-a-allowed."

He turned back to shoveling, but he did feel a good deal better. Some men had to be ordered to protect their wells. Other men, like him, didn't seem to have much choice when their heart closed around something. His heart seemed to have a mind of its own, and it was yearning for Naomi, the very least logical match in the entire community.

And these days, he was feeling dangerously close to falling for Naomi in a very real, very grown-up way.

Chapter Six

The evening slipped by, and the sun sank behind the horizon. Naomi worked alongside Mose as they finished with the stable, groomed the horses and then cleaned out the chicken coop. He kept telling her he could do it, but it felt wrong to make a man come do all that work by himself just because he was a man.

"It's not fair to make you work two jobs just because we're women," Naomi said.

"It's m-m-men's work." He frowned.

"*Yah*, but we can do it. Perhaps not as well as you, but—"

"It's m-m-men's work." He slowed the words down, as if that would make more sense to her, and so she'd let it go. He was sweet, and he was helping make their days around here a little bit easier.

"I really need to hire someone, don't I, Mose?" she said thoughtfully.

"*Yah*. Y-y-you do." He smiled, and his eyes softened, then he nodded out toward the corral. "Th-th-there's a l-l-loose rail."

After he fixed the loose rail, there was a damaged latch on a gate that also needed attending to, and Naomi was amazed to see Mose's nose for broken items around a property.

"How do you do that?" she asked him as he twisted in the last wood screw to hold the latch in place.

"Hmm?"

The light was low and soft, and somehow it made his dark eyes glisten. He looked down at the screwdriver in his hand, then back at her, and she couldn't help but laugh.

"Not that. It's just that you seem to know how to find everything that needs fixing," she said.

"It's all the same things, no matter who lives there," Mose replied, his words halting, but she didn't notice as much anymore.

"Like gate clasps?" she said with a smile.

"Yah." He nodded. "Plus, y-you closed it with a r-r-rope."

"Right." She shrugged, and a cool wind whisked around them. This was the time to head back to the house, but when she looked in that direction, she could see Aaron backlit in a window.

"C-can I ask you s-something?" Mose asked quietly.

"Yah, of course."

"Wh-what do I say to the woman Adel is having me meet?" He stumbled over the words, but pressed forward. "What do I say?"

"Anything you want, I suppose," Naomi replied.

"How do I…explain how I talk?" He dropped his gaze.

"You don't have to," she said.

He shot her a wry look. "*Yah*, I d-d-do."

"Adel will explain," she said.

"W-women think that I'm…not smart." He swallowed, and he stuttered when he talked, but the words came out. "When I was a teenager, I tried to ask some girls home from singing. One said it would be wrong because she thought I was mentally deficient. That stopped me for a while. When I was old enough to court and marry, I asked another woman home from singing. She was kind, but she said no. And I could see it in her eyes, the way she said it. She pitied me. I wasn't a man to them."

Naomi's anger rose up inside of her to meet his story. They rejected him… Mose, of all men! He was kind, intelligent, and ever so handsome. To think of a woman crushing him like that. It wasn't fair. He was certainly a man to her.

"Show them your column!" she retorted.

"That seems…p-p-prideful."

Naomi shook her head. "Maybe a little, but it would work. I'm sure Adel can show them your column. That would fix things. But, Mose, we all know about your column here, and you are very respected. Even the bishop wants your input."

"*Yah*," he said, "but the b-b-bishop isn't looking for a h-h-husband."

There was a playful twinkle in his eye, and Naomi burst out laughing. "Okay, okay, so a woman's perspective is a little bit different, I'll admit to that. But the right woman will see the man in you, Mose. Maybe *Gott* has been saving you from the wrong match by closing their eyes to you."

"Maybe…" He pressed his lips together, then nodded. "I n-never thought of it like th-th-that before."

"Mose, there are people who have married the wrong person," she said quietly. "I know one woman myself. Her name is Leah. She's deeply unhappy, ever so lonely, and very, very married. She's stuck. Maybe *Gott* is doing something special for you—throwing up obstacles in your path so that you don't marry the wrong woman."

"Lantz?" he said.

"*Yah*. You know her?" she asked, and her cheeks pinked. "I shouldn't have brought her up."

"I know Daniel," he said.

Naomi stared at him, then nodded. "Of course, he was from Ohio, too. You know him? You know him well?"

"*Yah*, he's from my community, and we're close to the same age. I worked with him on a barn raising, and he and I helped out an older couple when they got the flu and needed help at their farm," he replied, his words still halting, but far less noticeable. "So we talked a good deal."

"What does he say about Leah?" Naomi asked.

"He doesn't talk much about her," he said. "Not to me."

"He left her, you know," Naomi said. "Two years after the wedding, he just left."

"The b-bishops t-t-tried to h-h-help," he said.

"*Yah*, but it didn't work," she replied.

"Sh-sh-she didn't w-w-want him," Mose said.

"What? That's not the story I've heard." Naomi shook her head. "Leah loves him! He won't come home!"

She'd seen the look of misery on Leah's face. She'd seen how lonely she was, how she turned away when she saw courting couples. Leah was heartbroken.

"Sh-sh-she should g-g-go home to h-h-him."

"But their home is in Redemption," she said.

"Their h-h-home can be anywhere."

"But he was mean to her," Naomi said.

"He's not mean," Mose said haltingly, but his voice was firm. "Not Daniel."

"We're seeing opposite sides of the same story, aren't we?" she said. "There's always more than one perspective."

"Yah."

It was the kind of knot that the bishop normally took to Adel to help him untie.

"It doesn't always work out," Naomi said softly. "And that's the fate we all want to avoid."

"Yah." Mose was silent for a moment.

"Mose, I don't mean to scare you away from finding your wife," Naomi said.

"You d-d-didn't," he replied.

"Oh…good." She let out a sigh. "Because Adel would never forgive me for that."

She shot him a smile and he chuckled.

"So…" he said quietly, the stutter less pronounced now. "How do I show a woman that I'm a man like any other?"

What he really wanted to know was how to show a woman what he had to offer when the first thing a woman would notice was his stutter. She still felt her cheeks heating at just how transparent she'd have to be to answer the question. She'd have to tell him what she saw in him.

"Well…" She sucked in a deep breath. "You do it with your eyes."

"My…eyes."

"You have very nice eyes," she pressed on. "You have kind, expressive eyes. They are very dark, and you have long lashes. So when you look at a woman, you can…I don't know…show her what is inside of you with your eyes."

"I don't know how," he said haltingly. "I don't flirt."

"Well, you might need to start, Mose Klassen!" she said, and she reached out and snagged his sleeve. She tugged him around to face her. "You don't just look at a woman the way you would a barn or a horse. She's supposed to mean more to you than those sorts of things, and you have to express that."

"Like a horse?" he chuckled, and this time, the words came out smoothly. He was relaxing.

"You look her in the eye," she said, trying not to smile back. "Mose, stop joking, I'm serious. You have to look her in the eye—but not in the way you would when doing a business deal or greeting a friend at the store. You look her in the eye with some gentleness…"

His dark gaze met hers, and her heartbeat sped up just a little. His expression softened and a smile touched his lips. He had no idea of the power he had just in doing that one thing, and she hoped against hope that her face wasn't betraying her flustered heart right now.

"And?" he prompted.

"I don't know what else," she breathed. "That's all I had."

He didn't drop his gaze, though. He held it, and she felt her own breath getting shallow. He stepped closer to her, then his rough hand touched hers, and he closed his fingers around hers.

She should say something. She should stop this... He licked his lips, and she wondered what it would be like if he slipped his arms around her.

She found herself stepping just a little closer, and he ran his hand up her forearm, his fingers leaving a trail of goose bumps. His gaze moved down to her lips, and suddenly this wasn't just an experiment anymore. His eyes were filled with a combination of hesitation and longing, and she had the sudden urge to rise up onto her tiptoes and kiss him.

The sound of the side door opening surfed the night air toward them, and that seemed to break the moment. She swallowed, and they both stepped back. She turned around to see Aaron come dancing outside.

"Naomi!" he shouted. "Naomi! My *mamm* made cookies!"

"Aaron, back inside!" Claire appeared behind him in the doorway, and she made a swipe for the boy, but missed.

"Do you want some cookies?" Aaron called.

Naomi looked back at Mose, and she saw that his cheeks had reddened, too. She laughed uncomfortably.

"Do you want cookies, Mose?" she asked.

He shook his head. "N-n-n-n-no." That was all he could get out, and her heart gave a squeeze.

Stress clammed him up, locked up his words. What had just passed between them? Would she really have been so brazenly forward as to kiss this man? Her cheeks flamed at the very thought.

"Inside, I said!" Claire repeated firmly, and she pointed at Aaron and then into the house. The boy complied and went back in, and Claire shot Naomi a look laden with apology.

"You see?" she said breathlessly. "Use your eyes. You can say plenty with a look."

"Yah..." He half smiled, one side of his mouth twitching upward.

And even that boyish grin was plenty powerful, because her insides were already flipping.

"You'll do fine, Mose," Naomi said, attempting to regain her composure. "You'll do just fine."

Because if he could turn her insides into knots with a simple look, then other women would see it, too. He just had to believe in himself.

She met his gaze, and he nodded toward his buggy. "I sh-sh-should go."

"Yah. Good night, Mose."

Naomi headed toward the house and Mose went in the direction of the corral to get his horse to hitch up. She turned and watched him go, and he didn't look back at her.

She wished he would look back, give her some relief, take away the awkwardness and show her they were just old friends like they'd always been. She wanted him to set them back on the right footing again, but he didn't turn around, and she went up the steps to the house.

They weren't children anymore, were they? There were real, adult, grown hearts at stake, and hers was not so guarded as she'd thought.

* * *

Mose would have kissed her. That was the thought that dominated his mind as he drove his buggy away from the bed-and-breakfast…away from Naomi. What had he been thinking?

Because Naomi was all wrong for him. And if he could speak more fluently, he'd probably have told her exactly why and she'd never have been spending so much time with him. It was because his words got locked inside of him that he couldn't explain himself properly, although if she really did read his columns like she said, she'd see it, too.

All Mose had was how he looked at her—and that might show how he felt, but it didn't explain how he *thought*. A marriage was about more than a woman who could cook and a man who could work! It was about more than these simmering feelings that he couldn't quite identify but also couldn't quite deny.

Attraction wasn't enough. Tenderness wasn't enough… They were precious, but as lasting as a morning fog. A marriage had to have a firmer foundation than that!

And with all of that rattling around in his head, Mose still would have kissed her if Aaron hadn't interrupted with his piping little announcement about cookies. He would have leaned down and pressed his lips against hers…

And then what? Because he'd never kissed a woman before—ever! If he'd kissed her, it would be his own first kiss, and his emotions would get even more tangled up around her. His heart was not listening to his head, and standing out there with her in the twilight, his heart had been taking over.

Naomi had always been special, but he hadn't come to Redemption for her. He'd come to find a wife, and to help his uncle at the same time. But he was supposed to let his head lead and find a woman who would be a good match for him in personality, faith and her goals for her future. This was supposed to be logical!

That evening, his aunt was waiting for him with a mug of tea in front of her at the table as he came inside. He pulled off his boots and hung up his hat. He wasn't in the mood for conversation tonight, though.

"How are things, Mose?" Aunt Linda asked gently.

"Fine," he said with a forced smile.

"Just so you know, the tour map is different for tomorrow," she said. "Your uncle drew it out for you." She pushed a piece of paper across the table, and he picked it up. The map showed a route that went over to the river and past the icehouse, farther on to a sheep farm. It didn't go anywhere near the Draschel Bed and Breakfast, and his heart sank.

He'd been hoping to see Naomi tomorrow, but if the tour was taking him in another direction, and then he had the meeting with the bishop afterward, maybe it was for the best.

"You'll stop by the Friesen Looms sheep farm," Linda said. "You stay there for about an hour. They have a tour everyone seems to enjoy, showing how they shear the sheep and spin the yarn they use to make some really lovely blankets and sweaters."

"Ah." He tried to sound more enthusiastic than he felt, and his aunt didn't look fooled.

"Sit down," she said. "I was hoping to talk to you."

He sighed and did as she asked. He was her guest here, after all. She gave him a kindly smile.

"You always were a good boy, Mose," she said.

He smiled faintly in return. He was far from a boy now. "Th-th-thank you."

"It's harder than you thought, isn't it?" Linda asked. "This process of finding a wife."

"Yah," he admitted. "Much harder."

"You deserve a good woman," she said. "I know personally how complicated these matters can be. Did you know that your uncle and I had an arranged marriage?"

Mose blinked at her. "N-no. I d-didn't."

"Well, we did. I know what it's like to wait and wait to find the right person, and have it not happen the regular way. I wasn't beautiful, you see."

"No!" he said, quickly shaking his head. In fact, he found that hard to believe. She didn't look any different from any other woman her age.

"It's okay, dear," Linda said. "It's true. At least I wasn't beautiful in the same way as the other girls were. So a matchmaker started me with letter writing to a nice farmer's son—your uncle Abram—who was looking for a wife. We both wanted the same things, and we were both determined to love each other no matter what came at us. So we got married. We saw each other exactly four times before the wedding."

He didn't know what to say, and he dropped his gaze to the tabletop.

"Mose," Linda said. "My point is that it's possible for this to work. I've loved your uncle with all my heart all these years. I've stood by him, and we had six beautiful girls. With a wise matchmaker—and our Adel Knussli is a wise woman, I assure you—you can have the family life you long for. I promise you that. But you have to trust your matchmaker."

"I do," he said.

"I mean, really trust her," she said earnestly. "You need to trust that she can see what you can't. She's known the women here her entire life—you have not. She knows how they think, what they want, what they're expecting. She knows the family secrets, too, that no one would tell you about until after the vows. She knows more than you do about these women, so in order for this to work, you have to trust her guidance."

Mose wasn't sure how to answer that, but Linda seemed satisfied by the look on his face.

"Now I'm going to clean the kitchen," she said. "Your uncle will be back inside in a few minutes. He's not doing the chores, but he's a man of habit, so he's out there talking to the horses all the same."

Linda stood up and headed back to a sink full of dishes, and Mose slowly rose to his feet. He needed to trust his matchmaker. And perhaps he should also sit down and talk to her again. This wasn't an easy process, but it would be worthwhile if he could find his wife.

Yes, he'd go to see Adel tomorrow. He'd squeeze it in. He might be drawn to Naomi, but she wasn't the one for him. He knew it in the logical part of his mind. His aunt was right—many a successful marriage had been found through arrangements, and he did so want a family of his own.

Maybe *Gott* was trying to tell him something.

* * *

The next morning, there was a two-hour gap before the first tour group was scheduled to leave, so after helping his uncle with morning chores, Mose took his buggy to the Knussli farm. Jake Knussli was already out on the fields with his cattle, and Adel Knussli greeted him with a warm smile and beckoned him into her kitchen.

"Come in, come in, Mose," she said. "My sister tells me that you're relaxing a lot more in your conversation. That's wonderful to hear."

"*Yah*, it's h-h-h—" The word wouldn't come out, and he shut his eyes for a moment. Talking to Naomi was different than talking to Adel. "...helping." He said the word slowly, purposefully.

"I'm glad." Adel smiled. "Have a seat. I'll start some coffee."

Mose sat down at the kitchen table. It was damp still from being wiped down after breakfast, and he waited in silence while Adel put a coffee percolator onto the stove, and then bent down to stoke up the flames.

"I do have someone in mind for you," Adel said. "I haven't mentioned anything to her yet, because I have found in this position of matchmaker that I'm responsible for both the happiness of couples I connect, and also the disappointment of people who don't find that same connection. And I'd like to limit the disappointment, if I can." She came back to the table with two empty mugs and sat down.

Mose wasn't sure he trusted words to come out properly, so he just looked at her.

"In your letter, you said you wanted a woman who

was kind, gentle, sympathetic and a very good Christian," she said. "You also mentioned a quiet personality."

"Yah." He nodded.

"Lydia Speicher is all of those things," she said. "She's also tall, slim, and I think quite pretty."

He nodded again, unsure of what to say.

"She's quiet, too," she went on. "And I think she'd make any man a good wife."

Adel met his gaze, then pressed her lips together. "It's hard for you to talk to me still, isn't it?"

"Yah." He dropped his gaze. "I'm s-s-s-sorry."

"Don't be," Adel replied. "Is it easier to talk to Naomi? You two were friends as young kids. Maybe that helps?"

He nodded, and he couldn't help but smile ruefully. "N-N-Naomi is d-d-different."

"She probably talks enough for the both of you." Adel chuckled.

He shook his head. Because Naomi didn't. She did talk plenty, but she always waited for him to have his say. "She's f-f-fine."

"Are you ready to sit down with a woman you don't know?" Adel asked. "Or would that be too difficult?"

And sitting here in the matchmaker's kitchen, he found his heartbeat speeding up. This was why he was here—to meet someone. What was wrong with him that he couldn't do that? Why couldn't this be easier for him?

"I…I…want to." He slowed down, forcing out each word. "But…" He shrugged.

"Would you like a little more time to practice with

Naomi?" Adel asked. "We don't have to rush this, Mose."

He felt a burst of relief. Yes, that was true! What if he took a little more time, and then when he sat down with this lovely, eligible woman, he could make sure that he'd be able to actually talk to her. But more time with Naomi wasn't going to be as helpful as Adel thought.

"I h-h-hate this," he said.

"I know," Adel said sympathetically. "I'll tell you what. If you aren't comfortable enough to sit down and talk to a woman by the time you leave, then we'll set something up where you could write letters with her and communicate that way. That way, I could explain the situation, and you'd have plenty of time to talk things out with her. What do you think?"

Letters. Like his aunt and uncle had done. He could communicate just fine in letters.

Mose felt a smile come to his face. "*Yah. Yah.* Th-th-thank you."

The coffee had started to percolate on the stove, and Adel rose to her feet and headed over to take a look.

"There is a lid for every pot, Mose," Adel said, and she grabbed an oven mitt to move the coffee off the flame. "I'm determined to find yours. Do you trust me?"

Mose swallowed. This was the key, wasn't it? *"Yah."*

"Good." She came back to the table with the pot and filled his mug with steaming, fragrant coffee. "Because I know a good woman when I see her, and I might see more than you do at first glance." She put the pot onto a pot holder, and then fetched some cream and sugar and put them in front of him. When she sat down again, she filled her own mug.

Mose spent a moment doctoring his coffee to his liking.

"Many a Good Apple stays on the tree because it's too high to pick," Adel said. "And sometimes, it stays on the tree because it doesn't look quite so rosy, or because there were others that looked rosier at first glance and they were swiped from the branch first."

"Yah." He understood the analogy all too well. "I…I…like the idea of writing letters."

Adel smiled. She seemed to have noticed that those words came out more easily.

"Then that might be the perfect setup," she said. "Mose, I am confident I can find you a wife. And I don't say that to just anyone."

Even with his debilitating stutter? It had held him back for a very long time. What made her think her job would be any easier up against something so off-putting?

"You don't believe me." She waggled a finger at him. "I see it all over your face. But do you know why I'm so confident? Because my sister thinks the world of you. She thinks you're smart, sweet, dependable and truly decent. That combination doesn't come along every day, you know."

"Sh-she said that?" he asked.

"Yah, she did," Adel replied. "Now, just to be open and honest here, that situation with your cousin Klaus made Naomi very resistant to an arranged marriage. She has a few other reservations as well when it comes to a quick marriage, so I can't offer her as one of my

suggestions. But I do trust my sister as a judge of character, and she assures me that you are just as decent as you appear to be. With that kind of character reference, I know I can find a wonderful woman who'd be grateful to marry you."

Naomi was beautiful, energetic, outgoing. She didn't have to rely upon an arranged marriage to find her happiness, and Mose didn't blame her for having her own reservations about the process.

But for a man like him who was tied up into knots with his own words, it was his chance at finally having the family of his own he'd been longing for all his life.

"Will you find someone for Naomi?" he asked, his stutter still strong.

"Of course." Adel shrugged. "My sister is a wonderful cook, a warm friend, a kind neighbor. She's beautiful, too. Her problem was timing. There were more available girls than boys looking for wives when she was at that age. It happens to many a good person. I'm going to manage something for her, but I'll have to be subtler about it." She leaned forward with a conspiratorial smile. "You know our Naomi. She's stubborn, too. I won't even tell her when I'm setting her up. I'm just going to launch the appropriate man in her direction and let things develop on their own." She took a sip of her coffee. "But don't you tell her that, Mose. If you tell her, she'll be watching for it, and it'll never work. But when you hear of my sister's upcoming wedding, you can be sure that I'll be very pleased with myself."

Mose couldn't help but chuckle. He looked at his watch. "I'd...b-b-best get back."

He had a tour group to drive, after all. And after that, he was due at a meeting with the bishop and elders.

After a farewell, Mose headed out to his buggy. And in the back of his mind, Adel's words still rattled around. *I'm just going to launch the appropriate man in her direction and let things develop on their own.*

Adel wasn't launching him…was she?

No, she'd said he'd hear about her upcoming wedding.

He looked over his shoulder toward the Knussli farmhouse and he saw Adel smiling in the window. She looked so innocent.

But then he shook his head and flicked the reins. Naomi could do far better than him, and everyone, including her matchmaker sister, knew it. He'd be wise to stop mooning after Naomi Peachy now, before he ruined his own chances at a properly arranged marriage. Naomi might not want an arranged marriage, but he did.

It was time to take control of his own future.

Chapter Seven

The day seemed to wear on for Naomi. There were no tourist groups to visit them, and Naomi and Claire spent much of the day scrubbing the house from top to bottom. Naomi did laundry and hung it out to dry, and Claire scrubbed floors. Every time she heard the clop of hooves from the road, she looked up, hoping to see Mose's buggy pulling in, but it wasn't him.

Funny, a busy day of laundry and some baking was normally enjoyable. It was nice to have a break from tourists and just chat with Claire and play with Aaron as they got the work done together. And yet, that day felt strangely empty without a visit from Mose. And he'd only been around for a little while.

"Snap out of it, Naomi," she muttered to herself. Mose was meant for another woman—possibly even her friend Lydia. Now was not the time to start developing deeper feelings for the man.

That evening they held a basket weaving class for a small group of *Englisher* women who wanted to learn the skill from Claire, and then Claire took her son up to bed. A day well spent.

So why did she still feel a little empty? Was she just emotional today? Maybe she hadn't eaten well enough.

Naomi stayed up late that night, sitting in the soft glow of the kerosene lamp, an untouched sandwich in front of her, and her heart still feeling heavy. She could try and get around it all she liked, but she knew what her problem was.

"*Gott*," she prayed softly, "I want a husband of my own. I see my friends and family getting married, having babies, and I'm still alone. It's hard."

It would be easier to say that she didn't want a husband, but it wouldn't be true. She longed for a home of her own with a man she could love and cook for. She wanted a family of her own, and she'd been waiting for such a long time for *Gott* to answer the prayer of her heart.

"There has to be a man who can see what I offer and think he'd be ever so glad to have me," she whispered. "Someone who wouldn't be put off by my ideas. Someone who might even help me make a few of them a reality!"

Was she praying for an *Englisher*? She'd wondered that before. She knew a woman named Beth who'd left the Amish faith in her forties. She'd never married, and when she went English, she met a nice Mennonite widower right away who had four children and she was married within the year. Everyone thought she'd made a mistake by leaving the Amish way, but had she? There had always been a secret place inside of Naomi that thought Beth had done the right thing.

And yet, there was too much that held Naomi to the Amish way of life. She couldn't just leave. When she thought of being married, she imagined being a wife in an Amish home, living life their way. Leaving her faith was too big a price to pay—even to get married. Because when she imagined a husband these days, he looked tall, strong, and wore suspenders and a straw hat. And his face looked an awful lot like Mose's.

It was silly. His cousin had already sat down for an earnest talk with her and had all but run away. Mose was just as conservative as Klaus, and she knew what it felt like to be rejected so dramatically. It had dug right down to the tender roots of her pride. With Klaus, it had hurt. With Mose—

The thought of Mose looking at her honest heart and turning away was worse. She couldn't face that—not from him. She already knew she was wrong for Mose, and she'd learned the hard way not to take these things too lightly. When hearts got entangled, it hurt more than anyone imagined it would. If nothing else, that experience had given her new wisdom.

"Please, dear *Gott*," Naomi prayed. "Send me a good, Amish man who will love me. But I can't endure another humiliation like with Klaus and put myself out there for an arrangement. I need You to be my matchmaker. And *Gott*, I don't mind what You do to bring us together. Even if it hurts, I'm in Your hands."

She paused, her hands trembling. Then she added, "And please provide a wife for Mose. I know it's petty and small of me, but I feel jealous of whatever woman my sister finds for him. Take away my jealous thoughts and make me truly happy for him when my sister finds him a bride."

Besides, if *Gott* gave her a husband of her own, why couldn't she be happy for Mose? *Gott*'s blessings were broad enough to cover all of them. His blessings were not in limited supply.

The next day, Mose arrived with his tour group of energetic *Englishers*. Naomi had the pies lined up on the table, and Claire had whipped up a bowl of cream as a treat to go with each slice of pie. Aaron had the whisk, and was carefully licking every tong clean.

Naomi was working on her grocery list with her little pad of paper and a pencil. She tucked it inside her apron and opened the side door. She pushed the brick in front of the screen to hold it, then came down the steps and waited in a pool of warm sunlight.

Mose tied off the reins and then rested his hands on his thighs and looked over at her. A smile came to his lips, and relief washed over her. That was the old Mose again. Were they back to normal again?

He got up, hopped to the ground and went around to help an older man down from the wagon. The people were chatting and pointing at things—the fence, the stables, the horses… It never ceased to amaze Naomi how intrigued the *Englishers* were by ordinary things. But maybe it wasn't just a horse that pulled their attention, or a stable. Maybe they were drawn to something deeper—the simple faith that supported a simple life. Maybe they weren't seeing laundry on a line, but the hands that had put it there.

The Amish knew their lifestyle was special because

the very work that set them apart helped them to make everyday events an act of worship. Were the *Englishers* sensing that deeper act under the surface of a simple chore? Were they feeling the whispered prayer that had gone along with the work? Maybe they didn't know what made it special. Maybe they thought it was the simple life itself that held some sort of trick, instead of the prayer that draped around it, the blessing that settled over it. There was no trick—only *Gott*.

Claire appeared in the doorway and smiled her welcome as the people trailed in her direction and headed inside.

Naomi went over to where Mose stood and leaned against the side of the wagon.

"Hello," she said, looking up at him.

"Hello." He smiled again. "H-how are y-y-you?"

"I'm fine."

From the house, she could hear the murmur of happy voices. Their guests were having a good time, it seemed.

"Did you see the bishop yesterday?" she asked after a moment of silence.

"I w-w-went to s-s-see your—" He pressed his lips together, and his face flushed. "S-s-s-s..."

He clenched his jaw.

"My sister?" she asked. "Adel?"

He nodded. "I'm not going to meet the woman your sister has for me—" The words were halting, the stutter making the sentence much longer than it needed to be, and she could see the frustration in his eyes.

"Why?" she asked. Had he given up? Did he not like something about her? How did men make these decisions about women they'd hardly met? She'd been on the receiving end of a curt decision, herself.

"N-n-not yet," he said. He mimed writing on a piece of paper, and she suddenly remembered the pad of paper with her grocery list, and she pulled it out of her apron.

"No, I m-mean—" He shook his head, but then his eyes brightened, and he held out his hand for the paper and pencil. He scribbled something down and passed it over. It read: *Not yet. I'll introduce myself through letters first.*

That was what he'd meant by miming writing.

"That's not a bad idea," she said, but since he'd written his message, she added in the space beneath, *You write beautifully.*

Mose smiled at that, reached for the paper, and she watched over his shoulder as he wrote: *I'm better on paper.*

She reached for the notepad and replied: *Not true. I like you in real life, too.*

His smile slipped and he wrote: *You might not. I did go to the meeting with the bishop. It was about the politician who wanted help with the at-risk young people.*

"What happened?" Naomi said aloud. "Did anyone change their minds?"

Although by the look on his face, she suspected they hadn't. He shook his head, confirming her suspicions.

"Did they ask you what you thought?" she pressed.

Mose didn't answer, but he looked back toward the house, a frown on his face. Had he supported her idea or shot it down? She thought she knew.

"Just tell me what side you were on, Mose," she said. "You owe me that much."

He started writing again: *It's complicated. There are young people to consider, and the pressure on the community to take into account. I thought it was a risk.*

Naomi took the pencil back. *So that's it? They won't think about it anymore?*

He answered: *I don't know.*

But she did. They were never terribly warm to the idea, and now they'd decided against it again. Both the strength and the frustration of Amish living was in how little anything changed.

"We might be avoiding risk, Mose, but we're missing an opportunity to grow, too," she said.

He started to write and she leaned over his shoulder to see his words, her cheek brushing against his shirt.

To grow in numbers? he wrote. *We do need more people, more families. Are you thinking of that?*

Broadening the families available to marry into was important in an Amish community. Too much intermarriage between the same families could make certain illnesses more prevalent. Maybe she should have argued for that, but it wasn't what she'd meant.

"We're missing an opportunity to grow in here," she said aloud, thumping her chest. "In the story of the Good Samaritan, the church officials lost an opportunity to do *Gott's* will by avoiding the wounded man on the road. They walked past an opportunity to become more than a passerby, but an active help!"

Mose didn't answer, but he met her gaze soberly.

"We'll never agree about that, will we?" she asked.

He sighed, then wrote, *I think your heart is in the right place.*

But they still would never agree, and it didn't matter

where her heart was on the matter because the leadership wouldn't let her help. Not in the way she wanted.

Gott had blessed so many others with marriage and children, and He'd grown their families in the most beautiful ways. But *Gott* had not given her that blessing. Not yet. What He did seem to give her was a heart to help, and the one person who'd come right to her door asking for their assistance was an *Englisher* politician. That couldn't be a coincidence, could it? *Gott*'s hand was in everything. Wasn't that what they believed?

They see something in us, she wrote. *They see* Gott *in our lives, Mose. They just don't know it's Him that they're seeing.*

Mose nodded. *I agree*, he answered.

Then we need to share Him! she wrote.

There might be safer ways to do that, he wrote, and he looked over and met her gaze meaningfully.

"But the Good Samaritan wasn't thinking of his own safety," she said.

Mose put the paper down, and his fingers brushed against hers. "It's n-n-not my safety that w-w-worries me."

Her breath caught, and suddenly he looked just a little taller, a little stronger. He was a man, and it was his job to protect the women and children. That was the Amish way, and being under a man's protection could be frustrating when she felt held back, but also…her knees felt a bit weak.

"I can take care of myself, Mose," she said, attempting to lighten the mood.

"Y-you shouldn't h-have to," he replied.

The softness in his voice, the sincerity in his eyes—

she felt a lump rise in her throat, because if she had to be completely honest, she didn't want to.

But then the side door opened and the *Englishers* started to come back outside again, laden down with jars of preserves they had bought, and a couple of cloth bags filled with some knitted items that Naomi tried to keep in stock because their guests always bought them.

Naomi looked over at Mose again, and he handed her back her pad of paper.

"I'll see you later, I suppose," she said.

"*Yah.* I'll come do your chores," he replied.

The days were flying by. Mose wouldn't be here indefinitely, and soon he'd go home again and her days would go back to normal without him there to look forward to seeing. Somehow she was getting just as attached to Mose Klassen as she'd ever been as a young girl.

But Mose wasn't her little friend to do her bidding anymore. He was a grown man who had his own needs. He was here to find a wife, and when that happened, it would take him even farther away than the miles between their communities.

Mose drove the tourists back toward town again, the countryside slipping past the wagon. Behind him, the tourists talked softly among themselves as they bumped over some stray gravel on the road.

"It's beautiful," one woman said softly. "It's different out here. I wonder why…"

"I know," someone else said. "I can drive through regular farming country, and I don't feel this same sense of peace that's out here."

"Could you live Amish?" the first woman asked.

"No…it would be too hard. But I admire it. I think you'd have to be born to the life."

"Yeah, I think so, too. But it's special…"

Naomi had been right—these *Englishers* were feeling *Gott*'s hand over this land, and Mose adjusted the reins in his hands. But he had a little more experience with *Englishers*, having worked a few seasons of construction in a town near his Ohio community. People loved what the Amish had to offer, but the Amish peace, community and deep satisfaction came from generations of faithful living. It wasn't an accident or a gift that came without putting in the hard work, and very few people actually wanted to put it in. Like the women in this wagon. They wanted the payoff, not the challenge.

Mose had had work friends at that construction job who'd ask him advice, but they'd never follow it. Even when they got used to his stutter and communicating got easier.

"Mose, how do you find a nice woman like you Amish people have?"

But if he said, "You'd have to be Amish," they'd just laugh and carry on with their work, because they wanted a virtuous Amish woman without being a virtuous Amish man. Or they wanted to have the peace that the Amish enjoyed, not worrying about politics or the outside world, but they didn't want to fully give their lives to *Gott*, or cut themselves off from all those distractions that brought worry with them.

He'd see fellow workers carrying on with women at the local restaurants during their lunch break and ignoring text messages from their wives. Then those same men would tell him how great he had it as an Amish man because he'd get a woman who'd have a meal on the table for him when he got home. They didn't have that.

"Nag, nag, nag. She wants me to take her out, clean the house with her, go visit her parents… But I'm tired! I work too hard for that!"

But Amish men also worked incredibly hard to provide for their families and to allow their wives to stay at home with their children. Amish men prioritized their marriages and their relationships with their children. They didn't flirt with other women. They didn't make excuses to be emotionally distant from their children. So when they got home exhausted from a day of manual labor and that meal was steaming hot on the table, it wasn't out of sheer obligation on the woman's part. She did it willingly and with a full heart because her husband treated her like the treasure she was.

The benefits of an Amish life only came with hard work and dedication. There was no shortcut. So when a politician came along asking for Amish help to deal with *Englisher* problems, that put up Mose's hackles. They only had this beautiful lifestyle because they worked diligently to protect it, and from what he'd seen from many *Englishers*, they'd gladly suck up every benefit they could, and then wander off and not change their lives a bit. The Amish would be left with all the fallout of their precious community being ransacked for the gain of someone who wasn't going to benefit in the long run anyway.

Mose was right, and he knew it. But Naomi wasn't going to see that. Still, he hated that he couldn't be on the same side as her with this, because he knew that she was only wanting to do what was right. She was seeing the best in people, and maybe he didn't want to be the one to ruin that for her.

So that evening, after he'd dropped the tourists off once more at the parking lot, Mose turned the wagon around and went back to the bed-and-breakfast, even though he was tired. He mucked out the stable and filled the feeders with fresh hay. Someone had stopped by to see Naomi and Claire, so he didn't get to chat with her much. He just finished up, tipped his hat at Naomi, and hitched his buggy back up. She came to say goodbye, but there were eyes on them, so she stayed a proper six feet away.

"Thank you, Mose," she said quietly.

"Yah, yah…" He didn't want to try to say more. It wouldn't come out anyway.

"I do appreciate it."

He smiled back. She needed a worker to do this for her. He wouldn't be in Redemption for much longer, and he didn't like leaving her to all this work on her own.

Mose looked up at the curiously watching guests. They smiled and nodded. He wanted some time alone with her, but he had no right to ask for it, or to risk her reputation. He wasn't courting her.

"See you," he said, and he flicked the reins and headed back to his aunt and uncle's place. Maybe it was best to have some space to think anyway.

The next morning was Saturday, the end of the week for tours since they took Sundays off. This Sunday there wasn't a service. Every other Sunday was reserved for visiting family, and Mose's aunt and uncle were having a big barbecue with lots of family to come see Mose after all this time. He should be grateful, but it felt like a lot of energy…more so for him because every hello and chitchat about the weather was an exhausting effort. Still, he'd have to endure it. But first, he had one last day of tours for the week, and he hoped to see Naomi.

The day dawned crisp and clear. It was cooler weather than they'd been experiencing so far, and a few more leaves were turning yellow and orange on the tips of branches. It looked like fall would come early this year, and his mind was already moving forward to the farm work waiting for him when he got back home to Ohio.

The tour group that morning was made up of, among others, a small group of four women who seemed to be very excited to be out and about. There was a young married couple who only had eyes for each other, and one solitary, middle-aged man who sat right behind Mose.

"This seems like a decent job," the man said cordially. "Do you like it?"

"Yah." Mose nodded. He hated this part—the questions that he'd struggle to either answer or ignore.

He flicked the reins, and they were off, the horses plodding along and the wagon bumping over some pebbles in the road.

"You know, I told my wife I'd take her on this tour," the man said. "But I never did. I got too busy. And then she passed away."

Mose looked over his shoulder at the man, and his heart softened.

"I'm s-s-sorry," he said.

"Yeah. She was wonderful. She loved Amish country. She really loved your culture." The man looked around. "I can see why. Are you married?"

"No," Mose replied. "N-n-not yet."

Mose had the Amish clean-shaven face, which meant he was single. Only married men had beards, but this *Englisher* didn't seem to know that. And he wouldn't try to explain, either.

"Sweet on someone?" the man asked with a sad smile.

Mose felt his face heat, and the man chuckled.

"Don't waste time, young man," he said quietly. "You don't realize how much time you have together until it's over."

"Yah," Mose agreed quietly. "I'm t-t-t-trying not to."

He was trying to focus his energy in an appropriate direction—to get ready for an actual marriage with a woman who'd be a proper fit for him. He didn't know who she was yet, but all the same, he probably should stop wasting his time, shouldn't he?

The man fell silent, and the women pointed out some laundry on a clothesline, but their interest in the laundry wasn't the same as that of other *Englishers* who'd take pictures of it.

"We should really get a better clothesline on our farm," one was saying. "That one looks nice and sturdy. I think ours is too small to hold all the washing now we're running the farm together."

That was surprising—*Englishers* who used clotheslines? He snuck a peek over his shoulder at the women. They ranged in age from someone who looked to be barely out of her teens to a stalwart older woman with a wrinkled face.

"Grandma would be proud to see us women running the whole farm," the teenager said.

Their conversation moved on, but it became clear these women were related and were working together to raise cattle without any men involved at all. He felt bad that they had no men, but they didn't seem worried.

He reined the horses in at a four-way stop, waited for a car to go, and then flicked the reins, and they started forward again up a hill at their slow pace. When they crested the hill, he saw a car on the side of the road ahead of them with the hood up. No other traffic seemed to be on this road, and there was a teenage boy with a cell phone, and when he saw them coming, he waved his arms to flag them down.

Mose sighed and reined in. He couldn't fix an engine, though. He didn't know how they worked, so besides a ride, he couldn't offer much.

"Hi!" the boy said. Up close, he looked even younger. His face was smooth, and he wore a baseball cap pushed back on his head. His nose was freckled, and he wore a pair of jeans and a T-shirt with a skull on the front. Mose couldn't approve of that.

"Hello," Mose said. "C-c-car trouble?"

"Yeah, it's been giving me trouble for a bit," the boy said. "And my phone is dead. I need a new phone, too. How far am I from town?"

"T-t-t-ten miles," Mose replied. He hooked a thumb behind him. "Th-th-that way."

"Oh." His face fell.

"Give the kid a ride?" the man behind him asked.

Mose shrugged.

"It's a tour, though," the man said to the teenager. "According to the schedule, we've got another hour and a half before we get back to where we started from."

Mose was grateful for the man's chattiness. It saved Mose the trouble of trying to get the words out.

"I guess I don't have much choice," the boy said. "Can I hitch a ride, mister?"

Mose nodded. The only space left in the wagon was right next to Mose, so he scooted over to give the boy room to sit.

"Wow…" He grinned. "This is cool. I'm Trevor, by the way."

"Mose." He held out a hand. The boy looked a bit confused, but then took the hand and shook it.

Mose flicked the reins again and they started forward. Trevor leaned over to take another look at his car as they carried on past. Funny—the idea of *Englisher* teens in need of guidance was a little more daunting than a single teenage boy with a broken-down car. The boy just seemed…vulnerable. He postured, sat with his knees wide, tried to act like a big man, but while he was old enough to drive, he hardly seemed old enough to shave.

"I don't even know the address out here," Trevor said. "Can you explain where my car is so I can tell a tow truck driver?"

"Yah," Mose said. He could draw him a little map.

"Thanks." Trevor sighed.

"What were you doing out here?" the older man asked. "I'm Carl, by the way."

"I was trying to find a farm that's hiring for day workers," Trevor replied.

"Amish farms don't work Sundays, and you'd be in school the rest of the week. So you're looking for Saturday work?" Carl asked.

"Any day work," Trevor replied.

"Aren't you in school?" Carl pressed.

"I'm taking a year off."

Of high school? Mose looked over at him, and the boy's face reddened a little bit.

"I'm no good at school," the boy conceded. "I've been flunking out for years. You can drop out in grade ten if you want. That's what I'm doing. It's hard to find work, though. I was trying to apply to some farm work, and I couldn't find the farm."

"A whole lot harder to find decent work without that high school diploma," Carl said quietly.

The boy didn't answer that, and they fell into silence. This boy was looking for work, and around here, the teens who might get hired had been raised on farms. The competition was fierce. And Amish-raised kids knew the work better than anyone else. If a farmer had a choice between a green *Englisher* teen and an Amish-raised teen, he'd hire Amish every time.

"Do you know anyone hiring?" Trevor asked, looking over at Mose. "I'll do anything—farm work, manual labor, anything. I can follow instructions, so long as they're in English."

Did he know anyone? Yes, Mose did know someone who was looking to hire.

"It's not full-time," Mose said with only a slight stutter. "But I do know someone."

"Do you?" Trevor fixed him with a hopeful look. "Maybe my car breaking down wasn't so bad after all. Can you give me a phone number or something? What kind of work is it?"

"M-manual labor," he said. "C-c-cleaning out a st-st-stable."

Manure. Soiled hay. Back-breaking work. Was the kid interested in that?

"I could do that," he said. "Part-time is fine. It's a start, right? I've got to make some money to fix my car and get a new phone."

Had Mose said too much? Because he was only realizing now that he was all but promising to bring this boy to Naomi, and she'd get her heart's desire after all—an *Englisher* teen in need of help.

This was only going to fuel her.

Chapter Eight

Naomi lined up the jars of Amish peanut butter in a row, and then the smaller jars of jam went in front, glistening like jewels with the deep purples and reds. Then she moved on to some crocheted items. Today, she'd put them where the guests could see them right away, and she lined up some crocheted bookmarks, a Bible cover and several zippered change purses. Her fingers did the work as her mind wandered.

Mose was going to find a wife, and that would be a lot easier if Naomi also found a husband. But what kind of man should her sister even be looking for as a match for Naomi? A serious farmer wouldn't be right. Perhaps a fun-loving tradesman? How many single tradesmen in their thirties were rattling around in this area? Why did she have to be so different? Why couldn't *Gott* have created her to be calmer, quieter, and easier to match?

Because even the thought of this fantasy tradesman left her feeling a little empty and sad because she was still yearning after Mose. It was ridiculous of her, and she knew it.

"Naomi?"

Naomi glanced up to see Claire watching her with a worried look on her face.

"Yah?" Naomi said.

"I said, are we ready for the overnight guests?"

Naomi nodded. *"Yah*, we are. I made up the guest room already. In the meal preferences they said they need the food to be dairy-free. Did you get the almond milk at the grocery store today?"

"I did. And I think I can make some tasty scalloped potatoes with it, too." Claire cocked her head to one side. "Are you okay?"

"Yah." Naomi put the coin purse back. "I just hope these sell today. I know Lydia was hoping for the extra money."

Claire didn't seem to quite believe her, but Naomi wasn't in the mood to talk. Nothing could really change. She and Mose would never quite agree on any issue, and as friends it didn't matter so much, but in a romantic relationship, those little things became big things very quickly. *Gott* meant for a man and wife to be one flesh, not always battling each other.

"I saw Leah in town today," Claire said.

"Oh?" Naomi turned back.

"She's getting too thin," Claire said. "I asked her to come by for a visit, and she said she would, but I'm not sure I believe her. I think she's desperately sad."

"Yah…" Naomi's mind went back to their friend's tearstained face at Adel's home. "I think she is, too."

But there wasn't anything they could do for Leah's situation, either. They could just be her friends. Some problems were too big for even a community to solve.

The sound of horses' hooves and the wagon's wheels pulled Naomi's attention to the window. The wagon looked full up today, complete with a teenager in the front with Mose. She couldn't help but smile, and when Mose saw her in the window, she waved.

"Aaron!" Claire called up the stairs. "Come on down! The tour wagon is here!"

The drum of Aaron's feet sounded overhead. Naomi shot her friend a smile and headed for the side door. She propped open the screen as she always did, and headed down the steps.

"Welcome!" Naomi said brightly. "This is the Draschel Bed and Breakfast, and I'm Naomi."

The people started to dismount from the wagon. Mose hopped down and gave the last woman—the oldest—a hand down.

"I like your clothesline," the oldest woman said to Naomi with a smile. "We need one like that at our farm."

"Oh! They sell them in town at the farm supply store, I think."

The teenage boy stood by the wagon, looking around curiously.

"You can go on inside, if you like," Naomi said. "We have four kinds of pie for you to sample, and we don't mind a bit how many slices you eat."

She gave the boy a smile, and he glanced at Mose.

"Yah," he said.

The boy headed in the direction of the house, and she gave Mose a curious look. Did he know that *Englisher* boy?

"Who is that?" she asked.

"His c-car broke down," he said, his stutter not quite so bad right now. "He's l-l-looking for w-w-work."

Naomi blinked, looked over her shoulder as the teen disappeared into the house and then looked back at Mose in surprise.

"He says he'll do the stable," Mose added, his words still halting, but not quite as badly.

"And he'll work part-time?" she asked.

Mose nodded, and she felt a swell of gratefulness. Someone willing to do the work they needed help with… It was a relief, but more than that, he'd brought an *Englisher*.

"Mose Klassen, did you bring me an *Englisher* youth to work for me, against all your better judgment?" Mose shuffled his feet, and she batted his arm teasingly. "That is incredibly sweet."

"He needed work," Mose said quietly.

"And I need help. It comes together nicely," Naomi said. "He looks young, though. Shouldn't he be in school?"

"He d-dropped out."

Naomi let that fact sink in and she felt her eyes mist. "Mose Klassen, you dear man, you brought me an *Englisher* at-risk youth, to boot."

He shrugged bashfully, and if she didn't have guests looking out the window at her just then, she would have hugged him. Instead, she reached out and squeezed his arm.

"Thank you, Mose," she said. "I really appreciate this."

Perhaps they couldn't be the answer for every *Englisher* teen out there, but she might be able to help this boy…and get her chores done at the same time. *Gott* was moving here—she could feel it!

The boy's name, it turned out, was Trevor Wright. He needed a couple of days to get his car fixed, but he could start work on Tuesday, he thought. He'd be coming to do chores every afternoon for four hours, and Naomi would pay him an hourly wage and she'd teach him the ropes.

"I really do think *Gott* is working here, Mose," Naomi said before he drove away with his wagonload of tourists.

"*Yah*, *Gott* works in everything," he replied.

"Can I tell you secret?" she asked with a smile. "I asked *Gott* to throw a husband in my path, but instead he's tossed me an *Englisher* teen. I can feel it, Mose. *Gott* is up to something wonderful."

Sunday, Naomi visited with her sister and some aunts and uncles. Mose came that evening to help with chores, and again on Monday night. It was easy to get used to relying on Mose—he was so faithful to his promises. But those overnight guests were staying a few days, so Naomi couldn't just visit with Mose like she wanted to. There were beds to strip, food to cook, bread to bake, dietary restrictions to cater to—which was one of the biggest challenges. So she had to limit herself to bringing Mose Tupperware containers of sticky buns or slices of pie as her way of saying thank-you.

And then on Tuesday when Trevor was supposed to arrive, Naomi had a sudden sense of misgiving. Would he even come? Would he have lost interest over the last few days? Could she really rely on this boy?

He was due to arrive at four, and he arrived ten minutes late, to her relief. He parked his car next to the house and when she opened the door, he shot her a rueful smile.

"I'm sorry I'm late, Miss Naomi," he said. "I got stuck waiting at a railroad crossing. I'll know better for tomorrow."

"I'm glad you're here," she said. "Are you ready to get to work?"

He was dressed in an old pair of jeans and a long-sleeved shirt. He nodded. "Yes, ma'am."

"Just Naomi is fine," she said. "Come on. I'll show you the stable. And every day when you're done, you come on inside and I'll have something good for you to eat, okay?"

"Really?" He looked at her in genuine surprise.

"*Yah*, really," she said. "I will pay you once a week in cash. I imagine you need a bit of money in your pocket, though, so I will pay you every day for the first week just to make sure you have what you need."

"That would be great," he said with a relieved smile. "I've got to pay for gas to get here."

"*Yah*, I thought so," she said with a nod. "And every day you'll get something good we've baked."

"Thank you." Trevor grinned. "That's really nice of you."

She led him into the stable and showed him how to shovel out a stall, where to dump the soiled hay. He picked it up quickly, and he was a strong and energetic teenager, so the work wasn't overly exerting for him.

"You do this every day?" Trevor asked her.

"*Yah*. The animals need to be cared for," she replied.

"My mom doesn't think I'll be able to keep up with this job," he said. "She says it's way harder than I think."

"It's not easy work, but you get used to it," Naomi replied. "Your mother doesn't want you working here?"

"My mother wants me in school," he replied.

She could understand that. *Englishers* needed that diploma, and she could imagine a mother behind this boy, urging him toward better choices. Maybe she could help with that.

Naomi nodded slowly. "How well do you read?"

"I dunno."

"Come on, now," she said.

"Not good," he said, casting her an uncomfortable look.

"Hard to study when you can't read too well," Naomi said.

"Yeah, I guess."

"What if I helped you with your reading for half an hour after you finish work?" she asked. "Then you'd get paid, get something good to eat, and read with me for half an hour. Would that make your mother happier?"

"It might," he said.

"Well, you tell her my offer, then," Naomi said. "Whether you go back to school or not, you'll need to be able to read to get by, and I've got some experience in tutoring boys your age, so I think I could manage to teach you something. Besides, I need the help around here, and if your mother isn't supportive, I don't think I'll have you around for long."

"How come you're doing all this?" Trevor asked.

Naomi considered all the answers she could give,

but being an *Englisher* boy, he wouldn't understand many of them.

"I'm a Christian," she said. "And I care."

He just looked at her. His big blue eyes looked even younger in that moment. Just a blond-haired, overgrown kid. Her heart went out to him. *Gott* had brought this boy to her very doorstep, and He'd used Mose to do it. If this was the *Englisher* young man *Gott* had provided, then she'd do her very best by him.

"Now you finish up in here," Naomi said. "The fresh hay is over there. About three inches of loose hay on the floor of each stall is fine. When you're done, you come on back to the house. I'll pay you and have something nice for you to eat. You can take it with you if you need to get home."

"Thanks!" he said.

Naomi left him in the stable, and she paused at the fence, looking at the horses in the pasture beyond. *Gott* had given them so much, and blessings were meant to be shared. Somehow, her heart would not be soothed until she'd done just that with the *Englishers*.

It took Trevor three hours to finish the stable, and when he was done, Naomi had a thick roast beef sandwich and a bowl of soup waiting for him. She put a sticky bun into a plastic bag for him to eat on the way home.

Trevor sank into the kitchen chair in front of the food, and Aaron stared at him, wide-eyed.

"What's your name?" Trevor asked.

"Aaron," the little boy replied. "Are you gonna do the men's chores?"

"The what?" Trevor looked over at Naomi.

"He means the outside work—the stable," she replied.

"Oh." Trevor nodded and took a big bite of the sandwich. "Yep."

There was something satisfying about watching young people eat, and when he'd finished up the sandwich, the soup, and two muffins that she'd placed within his reach when she saw how hungry he was, Naomi went to the tin container on the top of the cupboard where she kept her petty cash, and she pried it open.

"That was three hours of work," Naomi said. She quickly calculated what she owed him and took the bills out of the tin and passed them over. "If you ever want to make a little extra, I can always find more work around here. Just so you know."

"Thank you!" The boy shoved the bills into his pocket. "So…same time tomorrow, then?"

"*Yah.* I'll see you then." Naomi smiled, and Trevor headed for the door.

She watched as he started his car in the lowering light, and then backed out of the drive. Somehow, she was already feeling protective of this *Englisher* boy.

"Is this a good idea?" Claire asked softly.

Naomi turned. "It all just came together, Claire. My sister said we could afford to hire someone, the congresswoman came to us, of all people, with her idea about helping *Englisher* at-risk teens. And then Mose brought this boy to our very step. It just feels…ordained. Don't you feel it?"

"I'm not so sure, Naomi," Claire said, shaking her head. "I'm sorry, but I'm not sure."

But Naomi did feel sure. For the first time in a long

time, she felt like she had more than a job to do—she had someone to care for. *Gott* hadn't given her a husband and family yet, but He had given her this *Englisher* boy for a few hours a day.

And deep in her heart she felt certain that *Gott* was using her to make a difference.

"She should have asked the bishop and the elders if they knew of any local boys who'd be willing help at her place before hiring on an *Englisher*," Aunt Linda said that evening, shaking her head. "I mean, technically, she can hire whoever she wants, but you'd think that for her business, having Amish help would just make sense."

"She's been looking," Mose replied, his words catching a little. "But it's my fault."

"*Yah*, I dare say it is!" Linda replied. "Naomi doesn't need more encouragement there, Mose. And you of all people know how important it is to protect our ways. Left to her own devices, Naomi would be virtually Mennonite within a year if no one told her no to something!"

"Your aunt is right there," Abram agreed.

They all sat around the dinner table, the plates already cleared away, with a pot of tea sitting on a knitted pot holder in the center of the table.

"In Indiana," Abram went on, "there was a family who wanted to help a homeless *Englisher*. They gave him a job, they gave him clothes, food off their table, and friendship, too. But the *Englisher* was an addict and his problems were bigger than they could help him with. He ended up robbing them to pay for his drug addiction, and he thumped one of their sons on the head on the way out. The boy got a brain injury and to this day, one side of his body doesn't work quite as well as it used to."

Mose stared at his uncle in silence. It was a horrifying story, and he didn't quite trust himself to words.

"The moral isn't that we shouldn't help," Linda said softly. "The moral is that we can't pretend we have answers that we don't. We're only people. Some interventions need to be left to *Gott* above."

"Yah," Mose said finally.

"Maybe warn Naomi about that," Abram said. "Maybe she'll listen to you."

She hadn't yet, and he was getting the gnawing worry that he'd just done something very silly and made things worse for Naomi instead of better. He wasn't even sure right now how it had all come about. It just tumbled into place.

That night Mose slept poorly, and the next morning, he drove two groups on various tours, and was set to drive a third group of *Englishers* that afternoon on their tour of Amish Country. This time, it was an employee group doing some sort of team-building exercise. They worked at the local grocery store, and Mose even recognized a couple of the women as regular cashiers. He didn't let on that he recognized them, though. He just gave them a nod, made sure they were all safely seated, and then flicked the reins.

Mose wasn't quite feeling like himself. He was normally a lot more cautious in his ways. He thought twice, even three times, and then acted once. He was at the meeting when the bishop and elders decided against helping the at-risk *Englisher* youth! What on earth had he been thinking in bringing Trevor to Naomi's bed-and-breakfast? The teen wasn't part of the political program, but he certainly was an example of an *Englisher* teen in need of some guidance. And maybe he understood what Naomi was feeling, after all, because seeing that barely grown teenager trying to act bigger and tougher than he really was had tugged at his heart, too.

"You mean they caught him more than once?"

The conversation behind Mose grabbed his attention and he began to listen in.

"Oh, they caught him three times! In fact, Vern didn't want to press charges the first time they caught him. They said he was just stealing food and Vern thought he came from a poor home. Never should have felt sorry for him. Then the second time, he was stealing gift cards—which is stupid because you have to activate them. So he just got a handful of plastic. So Vern didn't call the cops again. But this last time, he had enough, and called them in."

"When was that?"

"A couple of months ago," someone else said. "We know him on sight now. I'll point him out to you if I see him when we're working together. But you have to actually see him leave the front doors of the store without paying in order to call the cops. There are technicalities involved."

"So he's not poor, then?" someone asked.

"Even I'm poor!" one woman retorted. "I make minimum wage! I'm a single mom and I walk to work every day because I can't afford a car. You don't see me stealing anything. I pay for it honestly, and my daughter gets three square meals a day. That's no excuse."

Workplace stories. He knew what that was like.

They passed through the now familiar route, and then turned in at the Draschel Bed and Breakfast. Mose couldn't help a little thrill of anticipation at the thought of seeing Naomi again. Maybe he'd finally get a chance to talk to her some more.

As he reined in, Mose saw Trevor's car parked to the side. His passengers hopped down, chatting among themselves, commenting on the beautiful scenery around them.

The house side door opened, and Claire appeared in the doorway with a smile on her face. Trevor came out of the stable then, and one of the young women glanced in his direction, then froze. She elbowed the girl next to her.

"That's him!" she hissed. "That's the kid who keeps shoplifting!"

"Is it?" Another turned and looked, then nodded excitedly. "That is him. What's he doing out here?"

"Does he live out here? Why does he end up in town, then, stealing from our store? You'd think he could find someone else to rob out here…"

Mose's heart sank. No…not Trevor. He was the habitual shoplifter at the grocery store? Mose had brought a thief right to Naomi's door?

The employees whispered, looked over their shoulders in Trevor's direction, and headed toward the side door of the house, deep in conversation. Trevor's expression turned panicked, and he disappeared back into the stable.

Naomi came out of the house with a plateful of cookies in one hand, and when she saw his face, she sobered.

"Mose?" she said. "What's the matter?"

"We n-n-need to t-t-talk," he said.

Naomi put the cookies on the seat of his wagon, and he caught her hand and tugged her farther from the house and stable. This conversation needed to stay private, and they stopped behind an apple tree, the yellowing foliage shielding them from view.

"What's going on?" Naomi asked quietly.

"Th-the *Englisher* b-b-boy—" He cleared his throat. "He's…"

It took a couple of minutes to push past the words that kept getting stuck on repeat in his mouth, but he was finally able to tell her what he'd heard.

"And you're sure it's Trevor?" She frowned.

"*Yah*. They saw him," he replied.

"Oh, my…" she sighed.

"I c-c-can tell him to leave," he said.

"No!" Naomi's eyes flashed. "Are you really suggesting I tell that child that he's fired?"

"*Yah!*" he replied. "He's n-n-not a ch-ch-child, either."

"Not a child?" She shook her head. "I watched him eat like there was no filling him up! He's still growing, Mose. I doubt he even shaves yet! He's hungry, he's eager to prove himself and work hard, and you should have seen how proud he was when I checked his work last night. I'm going to help him with his reading, too."

"Naomi…"

"He needs help, Mose," she said. "And if he's made mistakes, then he needs a fresh start, too. What if he was your nephew? Would you have more sympathy for him then? We shouldn't be seeing our children and other people's children differently. There are all just children!"

"He's old enough to drive," Mose said, pushing past his stutter.

"Maybe so." She shrugged. "But he's not fully grown yet, and he still needs guidance, support and encouragement."

This woman was infuriatingly stubborn! Was she really going to argue to keep a known thief working on her property?

"What if he has bad friends?" he asked, the words halting but coming out, at least.

"I don't know." But she didn't look worried.

"It's not s-s-safe!" he said.

"I'm in no danger!" she retorted. "What is he going to do, thump me over the head and take my pots and pans? And get his friends to help him do it?"

A thump over the head was indeed a possibility, if Abram's story was accurate. And thumps to the head could be more disastrous than people often thought. And yes, he could very well bring friends to rob her home. Who knew how desperate people might get?

"Mose, I have something else I wanted to ask you— something I need to know."

Mose paused, waiting.

"You're going to find a wife soon, and I should think more seriously about getting married, too," she said. "But I'm thirty-three and still single, and I can't help but wonder if there's something about me—" Her cheeks flamed. "I mean... Mose, why did Klaus run from me?"

Klaus—logical, methodical man that he was—hadn't handled any of this well. If he'd changed his mind, he owed Naomi an explanation, either alone or with the matchmaker present. But he owed her that much.

"He—" Mose wondered how much to say, and the words came out haltingly. "He thought you were too strong for him. He imagined a different kind of marriage."

"Too strong..." He could see the hurt in her eyes. "Too mouthy, right? Too opinionated? Too laughing? Too happy?"

Mose caught her hand. "He wasn't right for you!"

"I see that." She dropped her gaze. "I'm not pining after him. This isn't really about Klaus. It's about... me. Whatever it is that keeps me alone." She sucked in a breath. "Okay, well, that's good to know, right?" She lifted her gaze to meet his, and he could see new resolve in her eyes. "If I'm ever going to get married, I might need to tone myself down somewhat...if that's even possible."

Mose hated that look in her eyes—the acceptance, the giving up. She was wild and free and smart, and— terrifying, yes, for a lot of men. But she was also a woman and capable of being hurt, and he hated to see the wounds under the surface. He didn't want her to change!

He had so many things he wished he could say, but even if he could say them without the stutter, he wouldn't know how to put it all together.

She wasn't the problem; the world that couldn't handle her was!

"No," he said, shaking his head.

"Mose—" She shrugged, and her chin trembled the tiniest bit. She was such a beautiful, incredible, intimidating woman. The Klauses of the world ran in fear. Mose wasn't afraid of her, however, even though he knew he needed a different kind of wife. But there was a man out there who would match her—and he'd be blessed indeed.

Mose stood over her, and her face was tipped up to meet his bewildered gaze. It was then he suddenly realized how close they were to each other, and her green eyes widened and her lips parted. She thought she was the problem, and that fact nearly broke his heart. For one rushing moment, all he could think about were her pink lips and the argument that was still whirling through his head, not quite coming together. He couldn't get the words out to do justice to his thoughts, though, so he did the last thing he could think of, and he slid his hand behind her neck, burying his fingers into her warm curls. He'd never kissed a woman before, and he had no idea how it was done. He wasn't even thinking about the logistics of kissing her, just of satisfying that overpowering longing inside of him to soothe the pain for her, and lowered his lips over hers.

That impetuous kiss was such a wild relief that it was like every thought seeped out of his mind, and all he could think about was the softness of her lips. He lowered his hands to her waist, and he felt her fingers tentatively touch the center of his chest. He wanted to pull her against him and never let her go, but he didn't dare... That would be too far. His hands on her waist, her hands on his chest, and their lips were the only parts of them that touched, but it was like the entire world swirled around them in that moment, and he wasn't even sure which direction was up.

Mose broke off the kiss with a ragged sigh, and he blinked his eyes open, his heartbeat skipping to catch up. Her eyes were still shut a moment longer than his, and he could see the tremble of her lashes against her plump cheeks, and when she opened her eyes, he felt a desperate need to explain himself.

"You d-d-don't need to ch-ch-change," he said. "*Gott* will provide."

As if that explained him kissing her without permission. She was wonderful, and somewhere out there, *Gott* had the right man for her. Why *Gott* was waiting so long to provide him, Mose didn't know, but he did know that Klaus was a well-meaning man, although not a terribly impressive one. If *Gott* made a woman like her, he would have made a man to match her.

The fight seemed to have gone out of Naomi, because tears suddenly misted her eyes, and she blinked them back.

"Mose, that kiss wasn't fair." Her voice shook.

"I just… I need to kn-kn-know that…that…" It wasn't only his stutter holding him back. His tumbling emotions wouldn't settle down and make sense. "…that you're okay."

He couldn't offer anything, and he knew it. That kiss had been impulsive and rash, but he wasn't even sorry for it, because he'd meant it. He was feeling things for her he had no right to feel, and he needed to know that when he drove away from here, she would be okay.

He had no right to step in here and kiss her like that, but on some level, Naomi Peachy would always feel like his.

"I am," she said. "I will be, at least. It's okay. I needed to know it."

Her fingers fluttered up to her lips, and he felt his cheeks heat. Maybe that kiss hadn't been fair...

Across the yard, the door opened and the guests started to come outside again. They were chattering and talking loud enough for them to hear the conversation where they stood by the tree. Trevor was seemingly forgotten, because now it was all about pie.

Naomi pulled away and shot him an agonized look before she turned and walked briskly back toward the house. He watched her dress ripple out behind her, a stray curl hanging loose down her back. That curl was probably his fault... He followed, but more slowly, and he stopped at the wagon. The horses stamped impatiently, ready to keep going. Their world hadn't just rocked on its axis.

What had Mose just done? His heart suddenly started to hammer in his chest as the magnitude of his actions floated to the surface of his thoughts.

He'd just kissed Naomi Peachy...

Chapter Nine

Naomi watched out the window as the wagon rattled out of sight up the drive, and she wondered if her hot face meant that she was flushed red. Mose had kissed her. She'd never been kissed before. In fact, if he'd given her any warning at all, she would have done something very awkward, she was sure. But as it was, there had been something between them that made the moment just…work.

And Mose—dear, sweet, handsome Mose—had kissed her. Had he been thinking about doing that for long? Did it mean he was thinking about courting her? She wished she knew what it meant! But he hadn't offered her anything. Maybe it had just been sympathy.

It seemed to shock him as much as it shocked her, though. Still, Mose wasn't the kind of man to do anything without thought and consideration. He was very serious, and he often wrote about the importance of thinking before acting, and not simply going along with a feeling. How often had she read something like that in one of his columns?

Did that mean he'd done just that—considered carefully his feelings for her and his hopes for his future—or did it mean that Mose wasn't practicing what he preached? He wouldn't be the first man in all of creation to set up an ideal and then miss the mark himself.

And yet, all Naomi could think of was the feeling of his lips moving over hers, his strong hands at her waist, and his heart thudding with the strength of thunder beneath her fingertips.

That had been a kiss! She'd waited thirty-three years to experience her first kiss, and somehow she'd thought it would be with a man she had a hope of marrying, at the very least!

"Aaron, why don't you bring these leftover cookies out to the *Englisher* boy," Claire said brightly.

"Can I have one, too?" Aaron asked.

"You can have one after you bring them out. He's in the stable. Off you go."

Aaron took the plastic container his mother held out to him and scampered outside, leaving the women alone.

"Another successful visit," Naomi said, attempting to sound normal. She reached for the plastic wrap to cover the pies.

"How is Mose doing?" Claire asked.

"He's—" She stole a quick look at her friend, but Claire didn't seem to be teasing or anything. "His stutter is improving a little, but mostly I think he's just getting used to pushing past it and getting his ideas out."

"That's a good thing," Claire said.

"*Yah*, I think so…" She turned away from the window. "He said before that he might try and get to know a woman through letter writing. It's easier for him to communicate that way."

"Will he write to you?" Claire asked.

"He…um…didn't mention that," Naomi said.

"He might have meant it, though," Claire said. "He's shy. He might not say things outright."

"He does with me," Naomi replied. In fact, today he'd done far more than speak—that kiss had sent her own mind for a spin, but she didn't dare mention it to Claire.

"You two share something special," Claire said. "You have childhood memories together, and you should see his face when he talks to you. He… I don't know…he lights up."

"Mostly, I talk," Naomi said with a rueful smile. And when she talked too much, he started feeling sorry for her. That stung.

"Well, then he lights up when you talk, and that's something special. He feels something for you—I know it."

"You had someone special once," Naomi said. "I know you don't like to talk about him, but…what was it like with him?"

"Joel was not who I thought he was," Claire said. That was more than Claire had ever said in the past, and Naomi crossed the kitchen and leaned against the counter next to her friend.

"Did he make promises?" Naomi asked.

"*Yah.* Plenty. He said we'd get married. He said he loved me more than anything and that he couldn't imagine a life without me." Claire shrugged faintly. "I guess that was a lie, because he most certainly has a life without me."

"Where is he now?" Naomi asked.

Claire shook her head. "No idea. He went to take a job in Indiana—there were farmers looking for help. He never came back. I never heard from him again."

"Did you write to his family?" Naomi asked. "Did he die?"

"He was just a travelling farm worker, Naomi," Claire said. "I didn't even know where his family lived exactly, except that they were in Indiana somewhere. It turned out that I knew far too little. Promises aren't worth much when you don't know the man behind them." Claire shot her a curious look. "Is Mose making promises?"

"No...no!" Naomi shook her head. "Not at all."

He wasn't promising to come back here. He wasn't asking her to visit him. He wasn't asking her to wait for him, or even asking if he could write to her. None of it. What kind of a fool was she for kissing that man without even a promise of the future?

"It's easy to get caught up in things," Claire said quietly. "I did, and I thought I was smarter than that."

"I think I can understand how easy it could be," Naomi admitted quietly. "I'm falling for him, Claire, but he's not asking for me, is he?"

"I don't know, though..." Claire sighed. "Mose does feel something for you."

"And Joel certainly felt something for you," Naomi said.

"You're right. It's good to be careful. We aren't spring chickens, are we?"

"Thanks for the reminder," Naomi said with a low laugh. "Mose says he's a bit worried about us, actually."

"Us, or you?" There was the teasing smile, then.

"Maybe me…" Naomi laughed softly. "For whatever that's worth. He overheard the tourists say they knew our new worker. Apparently, he's been caught shoplifting more than once."

"Oh!" Claire frowned, straightened. "Really?"

"Yah." Naomi sighed. "But it was food he took the first time. It seems that he was hungry."

"He sure ate last night," Claire said, and she walked to the window. "And he's eating again."

Naomi joined her at the window. Aaron and Trevor stood out on the lawn, and Trevor was eating the cookies in one big bite each, gulping them back like a hungry puppy.

"Mose is worried that he's not a safe person to have working here," Naomi said. "He wants us to be extra careful."

"Yah, of course, we will," Claire said. "I'm a mother. I'm always careful."

"I confess I argued about it a little bit," Naomi said.

"Is that why Mose drove off like that?" Claire asked. "You were arguing about it?"

"Did Mose seem upset to you when he left?" Naomi asked.

He'd been worried, frustrated with her. And then he'd been visibly upset when she'd mentioned Klaus. And somehow that kiss had been conceived of all their swirling, contrary emotions. That wasn't the way it was supposed to work, was it? But what did she even know!

"What do we know about him?" Claire asked.

"Mose?" Naomi said. What did she know about him now that he was a grown man?

"I mean Trevor."

Right. Trevor... That was who they'd been talking about. She'd have to get her balance back here before she made a complete fool of herself.

"Well, he's not going to school," Naomi said. "He has trouble with reading, and I'll be helping him with that, if he'll let me. He lives alone with his mother in town. She works a job at a hotel. That's about all I know."

"What about his *daet*?" Claire asked.

Naomi shook her head. There didn't seem to be a father in his life, at least not one the boy mentioned.

"I find it difficult to see Trevor as a danger," Claire said. "But we'll have to be careful all the same. Sometimes men can see things that we women don't."

"*Yah*...and the other way around, too," she agreed.

But her mind wasn't on Trevor anymore. It was slipping back to the memory of Mose's kiss—fired up and frustrated, yet tender, too. A thought suddenly occurred to her...

She had friends who had made life-altering mistakes, and she had to wonder, was she stumbling into her own? Mose was making no promises, and what they seemed to feel for each other was frighteningly powerful.

Would she be telling this as a cautionary tale one day to another woman?

Later that evening, Naomi served Trevor a hearty supper of beef stew and crusty bread and he did a few minutes of bashful reading with her. He struggled a lot with reading, and as she listened to him stumble over the words, she was reminded of Mose—so much intelligence all locked up. Trevor was a smart boy. He'd caught on to the outdoor work quickly, and being raised in town, it was impressive. But reading seemed to make him stumble, so much like Mose when he tried to talk.

Naomi pulled out some of Aaron's children's books about how a farm ran, and Trevor glanced over the page, his face flaming red.

"Just try," she said.

"It's a kids' book," he replied.

"Well…" Naomi shrugged. "Maybe you missed some of this when you were younger. There's no shame in it. We all have things we missed."

He shook his head and handed the book back just as Aaron came skipping up.

"I can read that book!" Aaron announced, and plucked it from Naomi's fingers. He opened it and started chattering off the words on the page, his eyes lingering only on the pictures.

"There you are, little muffin," Claire said, catching Aaron's hand. "Bath time for you."

Trevor watched Claire and Aaron go back up the staircase, his face still pink, all the way to his hairline.

"He's just had this one read to him a lot," Naomi said after a moment of silence. "It's memorized."

"This was a mistake," Trevor said.

"It's not a mistake," Naomi insisted. "We all start somewhere. I know it's hard. But the beginning of learning is letting go of our own pride."

"If it's all the same to you, I'd like to hold onto a bit of mine," Trevor said.

Naomi smiled ruefully. "You're clever, Trevor."

"I'm not feeling real clever today," he said. "I know you're trying to help. It might be better to just let me work and get paid. My mom is fine with me working here. Don't worry about that."

Naomi nodded. "Okay. Well, if you ever want that extra practice, I'll help you."

"I'll see you tomorrow, Miss Naomi," he said.

As quickly as that, her offered help was no longer needed. Why did she feel like she'd just failed him? Somehow, though, she had. *Gott* had sent this boy to her door, and it wasn't the wild success she'd been imagining it would be.

Naomi went to the door, and as Trevor's car pulled out, a buggy turned into their drive. Naomi recognized her friend with the reins in her hands. The sky was growing dusky, and when Leah reined in the horse and tied off the reins, she could see how slowly Leah was moving. This heartbreak had changed her.

Leah smiled tiredly as she walked up the steps.

"Do you have time for some tea with me?" Leah asked.

"Always," Naomi said. "Come on in. You look too thin, Leah. I'm going to tempt you with pie and cookies, too."

Leah smiled faintly, and she followed Naomi inside. She sank to a kitchen chair and let out a soft sigh. Leah looked older now—not just in the experience that was evident in her sad eyes, either. There were lines around her mouth that hadn't been there before. Anger simmered deep inside of Naomi's heart. No one should have the power to do that to a woman—no one!

"I'm glad you came," Naomi said. "I've been worried about you. But I didn't want to intrude if it was my sister you were wanting to talk to."

"Your sister has been through more than most have, so she understands," Leah said.

"You miss Daniel, don't you?" Naomi said.

Overhead Naomi could hear the soft murmur of Claire's voice, running water and Aaron's laugh. Naomi pushed the children's book aside on the tabletop.

"I do miss him," Leah said. "And I haven't been telling many people what's going on, because I kept hoping he'd come back for me. But he hasn't. I wrote a letter and his answer…wasn't promising. I decided it might be time to start being honest with people instead of using up my energy in pretending things are better than they are."

"Oh, Leah," Naomi said softly. "I'm glad you decided to share with me. We're friends. And in this house, we're all single. So we might understand better than your married friends do."

"Your sister pointed that out," Leah said.

"Good. She's right," Naomi replied. "This is what friends are for."

Naomi poured two mugs of tea and then went and got the leftover molasses pie and some plates. When she had a healthy wedge of pie in front of her friend, she took a seat again.

"You need to start eating again," Naomi said. "And doing things you enjoy."

"Like what?" Leah asked.

"Like visiting me!" Naomi said. "I should have come to you, though. I should have insisted."

"It's been a hard time," Leah said with a shake of her head. "You didn't make any mistakes. Don't worry. I'm the one who made a mistake in who I married."

"Yah?" How heartily was Naomi supposed to agree here?

"I think that is what it comes down to," Leah said. "And you're being too polite to say it. You know how our mothers warned us that our choice in husband would affect the rest of our lives? Well, I'm living that right now."

"Isn't there any way to fix it?" Naomi asked. "You did love each other. I think you still do love him."

"Daniel thinks I make him a worse Christian," Leah said.

Naomi frowned. "That's unfair of him!"

"He still thinks it," Leah replied. "He said he felt closer to *Gott* before he tried to share a home with me. But living with me, he's angry all the time, he feels far from *Gott*, and he says I just will not cooperate with him."

"Cooperate?" Naomi said.

"He wants me to see things exactly the way he does," Leah said. "And I don't! What am I supposed to do, lie?"

"Do you remember when we were little girls, we took a pact together that we'd never, ever tell a lie?" Naomi asked with a sad smile.

"And that very day, your grandmother made that chicken pie you hated so much," Leah said. "And you said you loved it."

"It was my *mammi*…and I love her." Naomi sighed. "You and I were two peas in a pod. That's what my *mammi* told me."

"Well, don't follow me down this path," Leah replied. "It's very painful."

"Did you have any warning that it would be this way?" Naomi asked.

Leah took a bite of pie and chewed thoughtfully.

"I knew he was much more conservative than I was," Leah said after she'd swallowed. "But I thought that we would find our own way. I thought he'd appreciate my thoughts and how I see things. I thought I might bring him some joy because he seemed so...serious."

This was feeling very familiar.

"Daniel thought that after we married, I'd change, and honestly, Naomi, I tried to! I tried to be the woman he wanted, but I couldn't keep up!"

"Why would he want you to change?" Naomi asked, shaking her head. "You were always such a ray of sunlight in a room. Your laugh, your jokes, your fresh way of seeing things...to have a husband who didn't appreciate your greatest strengths would be awful."

"*Yah*, it's been hard. Maybe it was my own pride, but I thought I'd be a wonderful wife."

"You are a wonderful wife!" Naomi said. "I'm sorry he doesn't see it right now."

"I know the marriage was fast and arranged," Leah said, "but when I gave him my vow, I gave him my heart, too. I meant it with every atom of my being. I know he's disappointed in the wife I turned out to be, but for better or for worse, we're married. But when he said that I made him a worse Christian—" Her voice broke.

"That was as much as you could take?" Naomi said softly.

Leah nodded. "They say everyone has a limit of what they can endure. But you don't know your own until you're past it, and then you see it behind you. And that was mine. I said if he wanted to go back to Ohio, he should go."

"Is it possible that he was saying something that sounded cruel, but he didn't mean it quite the way he said it?" Naomi asked.

"Is he here?" Leah spread her hands, then sighed. "He meant it. It broke my heart, and I simply have to accept it. That's why I'm telling you the worst. I'm tired of trying to hide what happened. At least if you know, I can start accepting that he doesn't love me."

"Oh, Leah…"

"No, don't give me pity. Then I'll get all teary. I'm ready to face this, Naomi. I need to build a life for myself without him. Because I'm not going to be his wife in his home. That's gone."

"Okay. No pity, then," Naomi said.

Leah licked her lips. "I'm going to find a business I can run. Like you're doing with your sister's bed-and-breakfast." Her face colored. "I'm not saying you'll be single like me, but I admire what you're doing."

Naomi batted her hand through the air. She didn't take offense that easily, but Naomi might very well stay single, all the same.

"What sort of business would you start?" she asked.

"I don't know," Leah said. "Maybe I'll open a shop, or start up some sort of tourist attraction. I've got to put my mind into it and figure it out. But it's time to stop being sad and start building my life back."

"You make delicious chocolates," Naomi said.

"*Yah*, those are fun to make." Leah shrugged. "I had an idea to make some hard candy sticks—different flavors."

"That's a good idea," Naomi said. "I'd help in any way you wanted. We could even sell some here. We already sell Lydia's crochet items, and the tourists love them." Naomi nudged Leah's pie toward her. "But do me one favor in return."

"*Yah?*" Leah looked over at her uncertainly.

"Eat. You need to get your strength back, and your laugh. My personal theory is that it starts with pie."

Leah smiled then, and for the first time it seemed to touch her eyes. "I think I'll be okay, after all, Naomi."

"You have us," Naomi said. "We'll make sure you're okay!"

Leah took a bite of pie, and then another. And after about ten minutes, she'd cleaned her plate, and without a word, Naomi dished another piece of pie onto her plate with a wink. Claire came down the stairs and she shot Leah a smile.

"Leah! It's nice that you came by," Claire said, and she came to the table to join them.

Leah's smile shone a little bit brighter as the three women talked about sticks of candy and tourists' tastes, and polished off the last of the pie. Sometimes, it wasn't about solving a problem so much as sharing the burden together. Leah was going through some hard times, and she might have regrets for the rest of her life, but she also had a community to hold her up and keep her moving forward.

Yet, as Naomi watched her friend struggle to smile

and laugh again, with that sadness deep in Leah's eyes, Naomi was also remembering Mose's kiss…

Some men were easy to love, but harder to please. Naomi would do well to remember Leah's pain, because Naomi and Leah had always been those two peas in a pod. They were very much alike, even in the kind of men that they fell for. If Naomi didn't want to end up heartbroken and lonesome, even in marriage, then she had to learn from her friend's mistake.

Chapter Ten

That night, Mose lay awake in his aunt and uncle's guest bedroom, the window cracked open so that a chill breeze worked its way inside and cooled the whole room. He was still remonstrating himself for what he'd done that day... He'd kissed Naomi! He hadn't planned it—it wasn't like he'd been trying to find a way to kiss her. But it wasn't like he'd never thought about it before, either.

When he was a little boy, he'd loved plum jam, and whenever his mother made it, she told him not to touch the jars. One year, he could think about nothing else for days, and then when his mother left the kitchen, he reached out and grabbed a jar. It was piping hot and burned his fingers badly.

Why had he grabbed it? It was silly—he'd even known it was hot! It was just that he'd thought about it so much that he found himself doing it without thinking it through, and this kiss felt like it fell under the same category.

He knew he had no right to kiss her like that. He

knew it was out of line, and inappropriate. But he'd been thinking about her so much, even letting his mind wander down the road of what it would be like to kiss her, that when he found himself looking down into her teary eyes, he'd done it.

The Bible said that out of the abundance of the heart the mouth speaketh, and it seemed to be that out of the abundance of his own heart he'd kissed her, too. He was supposed to have more self-control than that. And now, lying in bed, he felt like a fool...because even though he knew he had to face Naomi again, he couldn't help but remember what her lips had felt like against his...

She'd tasted like honey.

The next day, Mose attempted to put his attention into his tours, but even so, his tourists wandered off and got entranced by some cattle in a field, which set him back half an hour and he got his morning tour group back late, and the next group of bustling, excited people was already milling about and ready to leave.

"I'm sure Naomi will feed you," Linda said with a reassuring smile. "This is your last day driving for us, Mose. We really appreciate all you've done."

His last day...and then he'd head back to Ohio, back to his regular life. He'd write some letters and see if perhaps a woman might see her way to marrying him.

He should be looking forward to this. It was the next step in getting the life he'd been longing for. But somehow, the only woman on his mind these days was Naomi Peachy.

"Yah," he agreed. "Sh-she will."

But this also meant that he was going to have to

go inside and face Naomi. Would she have told Claire about that kiss?

He sincerely hoped not! But he also knew that the best way to live was so that anything a man did could be talked about openly. Then there was no fear of gossip. If he didn't want her to tell others that he'd kissed her, he shouldn't have done it! It wouldn't be her fault if she told the whole world.

The tourists climbed up into the wagon, talking excitedly to each other, and settled into the bench seats. Then Mose gave his aunt a nod goodbye, flicked the reins, and the horses started forward again.

When Mose arrived at Draschel Bed and Breakfast that afternoon, his stomach was rumbling. He reined in the horses and helped his passengers disembark. He stood there for a moment, waiting to see what would happen, and the side door opened, but instead of Claire waiting to welcome in the guests, it was Naomi.

Maybe she didn't want to see him alone again, and he felt his face heat at the thought. He'd have to explain himself—if he could even get the words out. He should have written something that she could read later, but he hadn't thought of it.

Naomi met his gaze and angled her head into the house in invitation. He'd explain himself somehow. He followed the rest of the *Englishers* up the steps and into the fragrant kitchen.

Naomi cast him a smile and handed him a plate with a large slice of molasses pie without a word to him.

"Welcome, everyone," she said cheerily to the *Englishers*. "As you can see, we have several kinds of pie for you to sample today. If you haven't tried our traditional molasses pie, I encourage you to take a slice. It is just delicious, and if you want to tell your friends that you had some authentic Amish baking, that will do it!"

Several of the tourists went toward the molasses pie, and Mose took a big bite of his own slice, watching Naomi as she served her guests. Claire was nowhere to be seen, and he glanced around, looking for signs of the boy, but all was quiet.

When the tourists had settled into eating, Naomi came over to where Mose stood. She settled next to him against the counter and glanced up at him from the corner of her eye. She was embarrassed, too.

"I owe you an ap-ap—" His stutter was strong and he couldn't get the last word out.

"It's okay," she said quietly.

He had so much he wanted to say—how he wished he'd behaved better yesterday, and how kissing her had been a wild relief, but he wouldn't make his feelings her responsibility. He wanted to tell her that he wouldn't do it again, and that she could be around him and not be afraid that he'd overstep like that again. But when he looked over at her, she met his gaze, then she shrugged.

"It really is okay," she said.

He nodded. "Okay."

Times like this one, he wished he could just say what was in his heart, but it had always been like this. Maybe he would write to Naomi after he got back, and he'd say it better than he could even now in the moment, and somehow clean up the mess he'd created. He took another bite of pie.

"Claire took Aaron to play at a neighbor's house this afternoon," Naomi said after a moment of silence. "This morning, he announced that he was the most handsome boy in all the world, and Claire said that was quite enough of that, and he'd better spend some time with other boys to see that they were all equally special."

Mose chuckled, chewing.

"It's not easy raising an Amish child around this much attention," Naomi said. "The *Englishers* spoil him too much."

"Yah," he agreed, swallowing. But what were they supposed to do? *Englishers* raised children differently. They gave them lots of individual attention and praised them constantly. Amish children didn't expect that kind of lavish praise, even after hard work, so when they received it, it was bound to cause some confusion.

"You're alone, then?" he asked, the words halting as he spoke.

"Yah." Her gaze flowed over the room full of *Englishers*. "It's fine. Trevor is already working in the stable. I've been paying him daily to start, because he has to pay for gas to get here and all that. It can't be easy."

She was thoughtful, and he wasn't sure if Trevor would appreciate that or not. Teenagers didn't usually realize how precious that was when someone considered their needs and comfort. When he was a teen, he certainly hadn't.

"Excuse me, are you selling this jam?" one of the women asked. "I'd love to buy some. Is this strawberry mint jam? I've never tried it. It sounds delicious."

"Yes, I am!" Naomi crossed the kitchen and took down a money box.

Naomi told her the prices, and the other guests clustered around, pulling out their wallets. Naomi smiled, opened the money box, and then he saw her expression change. She looked confused, closed it, opened it again, then seemed to shake it off as she accepted money and made change for her customers.

"Wh-what's wrong?" he asked her quietly when she'd finished selling the last of the jams.

"I thought I had two hundred dollars in this box," she said quietly. "There's only a bit of change now—some small bills and coins."

"Are you sure?" he asked.

"*Yah*. I'm very careful with this money. I have to account for every cent to my sister once a week."

Missing money and a shoplifting boy helping with the chores.

"T-T-Trevor?" he asked.

"No!" Naomi paused, then shook her head. "No, I would never assume something like that. I'll recheck my books. Maybe I forgot something."

He doubted it. Naomi wasn't the absentminded type. And by the look on her face, the discrepancy worried her. This was what he'd been concerned about—Naomi's kindness being taken advantage of. She didn't deserve this, and she might not have a man here to stand up for her, but in this very moment, she had him.

Naomi sighed. "I feel bad, though, because I obviously can't pay him today in cash like I wanted to."

"H-here." Mose pulled a small roll of bills from his pocket and handed a few over.

"Mose, no!" she said. "I can't take this from you!"

"It's fine," he said, and he pressed the bills into her hands.

She nodded. "I'll pay you back, Mose. I'm going to

the bank tomorrow morning, and I'll have the money for you tomorrow. That's a promise."

He didn't need to be paid back, but the tourists were starting to look antsy. Their pie was eaten, their jams purchased.

"I need to show them Lydia's crochet items," Naomi said, casting him an apologetic look. She gestured toward the sitting room and raised her voice. "We have a few craft items, if you'd like to take a look. There are some scarves and mittens that my own sister made, and some really gorgeous crocheted items made by my dear friend Lydia. Feel free to come take a look." She glanced back at Mose and added in Pennsylvania Dutch, "Thank you, Mose. You're such a good friend."

A friend. Yes, that was what he was supposed to be with her, but it was hard to keep that line clear in his own head these days. Mose finished his pie and put the plate in the sink. He looked out the window and saw Trevor disappear back into the stable. He paused, thinking... Maybe he'd just go out and see the kid, see how he was doing. Maybe all would be fine, and it would put his mind at ease.

He put his hat back on his head and went out the side door. His horses, still hitched up, ate from their feed bags, shuffling their hooves in the gravel. A rooster crowed from the neighbor's farmyard, and another from farther away answered it.

It was a quiet afternoon, and when Mose pushed open the stable door, he found Trevor mucking out a stall. The boy straightened.

"Hi," Trevor said. His nose looked sunburned. He needed a hat with a brim.

Mose gave him a nod, and the boy turned back to his work.

"I should probably thank you for hooking me up with this job," Trevor said. "I always wanted to work on a farm or something, but growing up in town, I wasn't sure I'd get the chance."

"Yah..." Mose looked around. The boy's work was adequate—not pristine, but he didn't have much experience, either. One stall that had been finished with new hay still had some remnants of dirty hay in one corner. That was a detail an Amish boy wouldn't miss. "You n-need a h-h-hat."

"Yeah, probably," Trevor said. "I've got one at home. I forgot to bring it today."

Mose nodded again, and as Trevor came out of the stall, Mose saw a couple of bills poking out of his back pocket. The boy leaned down to grab something, and the bills pushed up, so that when he stood upright again, one fell out.

Cash. Mose's heart sank. He hadn't been hoping to find it this way... Trevor wheeled the full barrow toward the back door and Mose picked up the bill.

"T-T-Trevor," he said.

He turned, spotted the bill, checked his pocket and pulled out the rest. It looked to be approximately two hundred dollars. Trevor took the bill back.

"Thanks," Trevor said. "I don't want to lose that."

No one wanted to lose that kind of money, but Mose was amazed at how smoothly the boy retrieved the cash and pocketed it again. No guilt on his face. No pause in his pace.

"You should give that back," Mose said quietly. His stutter was there, but not as bad as it could have been.

"What?" Trevor looked over at him.

"Sh-she hired you. Sh-sh-she deserves b-b-better."

"What?" Trevor repeated, his brow furrowing, but realization of what Mose was saying seemed to be dawning on him.

"G-give it back to N-N-Naomi," Mose said. Trevor would feel better when he did. *Gott* never blessed a thief, and whatever money Trevor stole would only run through his fingers anyway.

"You think I took this from Naomi?" Trevor shook his head. "Seriously?"

Mose didn't answer, but he fixed the boy with a solemn look, praying silently that Trevor would do the right thing.

"You think I stole this," Trevor said when Mose hadn't said anything, and the boy's voice shook. "Right. Right. Of course, because it's not possible that I have money for any legitimate reason, is it? I'm just some poor kid from the wrong side of the tracks, and anything I have must belong to someone else, right?" Trevor was trembling now. "Who says I'm a thief? Huh?"

Mose's words were blocked up inside of him now, not that he'd say where he'd heard it.

"The people from the grocery store, right?" Trevor said. "They said stuff about me, and you believed it! No one asked me, did they? You never asked me! Miss Naomi never asked me!"

"D-do the r-right thing," Mose said. Whatever that was! But yes, people had talked. Reputations followed a man, and maybe it was time Trevor learned that lesson.

"I didn't steal this money," Trevor said, shaking the bills at Mose. "But obviously that doesn't matter to you, either! This is money to pay the last of what I owe to the mechanic who fixed my car. My mom wants me to pay him on my way home so I don't owe him anything!"

He threw down the shovel and pushed past Mose, heading toward the side door.

"I don't need this job," Trevor said bitterly, and the door bounced shut behind him. A moment later, Mose heard an engine start, and the spin of wheels.

He'd messed that up. He hadn't meant to chase the boy off, just to talk about it—maybe give him some advice, show him how to make things right. But nothing could be made right if Trevor was going to dig his heels in.

But there was a stall still left to clean, and Mose picked up the shovel. He'd finish the work while he waited on his tourists. At the very least, Naomi's stable would be cleaned out this afternoon, and then he'd have to explain himself.

Naomi was pleased that several more craft items sold that day. One pair of mittens, two scarves, a crocheted shawl, and six crocheted Christmas tree ornaments. Lydia would be very happy to get her part of the sales money, too.

When the tourists left her home, she noticed that Trevor's car was gone. He hadn't come in to be paid, and that was strange. Mose came out of the stable, and he pulled off some work gloves and brought them over to her.

"I f-f-finished up in there," he said.

"Why were you doing it? Where's Trevor?"

The tourists seemed ready to leave. They were milling around the wagon, waiting to be let back up, and Mose's gaze flicked between her and the wagon.

"He...left." Mose pressed his lips together. He looked upset—angry?

"Without finishing his work," she said. Was that a guilty conscience? The missing money, her new employee who left in the middle of work. Her heart sank.

"He had cash on him," Mose said quietly.

"How much?"

"I didn't count it," he said, the words catching and taking extra time to come out. "But it looked...suspicious."

"Oh, Trevor..." She rubbed her hands over her face. "I didn't want it to be him, Mose."

"I know."

She looked up at him and sighed. "Thank you for finishing up out there. I appreciate all of this."

Mose just shrugged it off.

"You go home soon, don't you?" she asked.

"T-t-tomorrow."

As soon as that. The hard thing was, Mose's visit had shown her how nice it felt to have a man to lean on. And as quickly as she'd seen what she was missing, he was leaving again.

"Come back for dinner?" she asked hopefully.

"Yah." He nodded and smiled back, looking relieved. *"Yah..."*

Trevor had stolen from her. That realization was growing heavier and heavier inside of her. The boy she thought *Gott* had brought to her for a purpose, who was supposed to benefit from a Christian environment, had taken her money.

When had he done it? Was it when she'd gone out to trim back the raspberry bushes in the front of the house? Or maybe when she'd gone upstairs to clean… When had Trevor done it?

"I'm sorry," Mose said. "I didn't want to be right."

"You didn't do it, Mose," she said. "Besides, maybe *Gott* will use this yet. Maybe Trevor will come back and apologize. Maybe he'll need to see what forgiveness feels like."

Mose cast her a long-suffering look, and then nodded in the direction of the wagon.

"Yah, yah," she said. "See you at supper."

He smiled and headed over to the wagon, where his tourists were already loaded up and ready to go. He hoisted himself into the seat and gave her one last smile before he flicked the reins.

She'd miss Mose when he was gone. Life's complications were easier to bear with him around. The wagon disappeared behind the trees onto the road, and Naomi turned back into the silent house. It was time to clean.

Mose arrived back at the house just as she was pulling the cinnamon buns from the oven. She mixed up a bowl of icing with one hand as she glanced out the window, watching as he unhitched his horses. He looked up, saw her in the window and a smile broke over his face. Her heartbeat sped up at that smile, and she found her cheeks heating.

Mose Klassen was too handsome for his own good.

A few minutes later, Mose tapped on the door, then pushed it open.

"Come on in, Mose," Naomi called.

He pulled off his hat and smoothed his hair down with the other hand, looking over at her a little uncomfortably.

"All the way in," she said with a chuckle. "Claire and Aaron aren't back yet. I'm not sure if they stayed for supper at the Wegmans' place, or if they're coming back. It might be just you and me."

"I w-w-won't mind," he said.

Naomi dropped her gaze. Honestly, neither would she.

"I'm sorry about Trevor," he said quietly, his stutter sprinkled through his words. "I feel responsible. I couldn't say what I wanted to say to him. I wanted to tell him how to make it better. I wanted to explain how to apologize to you. If I could have said it, it might be fixed by now."

"No, no," Naomi said, shaking her head. "You can't blame yourself. If he stole from me, then he stole. *Gott* will have to work on his conscience. That's not your job, Mose."

Mose didn't look any cheerier about it, though, and she didn't feel any better, either.

"I'm surprised he did that, though," she admitted. "I was paying him daily to help with his expenses. I'd offered to help him with his reading, and that didn't really go very well…"

"What h-h-happened?" he asked.

"He needs a lot of help in reading," she said. "More than a bit of practice. I took out a children's book, and it offended him." She swallowed. "You don't think that's why he stole from me, do you?"

Mose just shook his head.

"I really wanted to give him a chance, Mose," Naomi said quietly. "I really did think that *Gott* used you to bring him to my door. I wanted to make a difference for that young man, but I suppose people don't easily fit into our fantasies about helping them, do they?"

"No, they don't," he agreed.

"Still…" She shrugged sadly and looked down at the bowl of icing.

Outside, Naomi heard another buggy, and she looked out to see Claire returning. It looked like they wouldn't get their dinner alone, after all. Maybe it was better this way—less temptation for her to feel like their relationship was closer than it was.

"Claire's here," she said.

Mose didn't answer, but he did catch her eye, and she saw regret in his dark gaze.

"This isn't your fault, Mose," she said. "You just caught him."

When the side door opened, Aaron came bounding inside. He went up on his tiptoes to drop his hat onto a peg and came up to the counter.

"What's for dinner, Naomi?" he asked.

"Pork," Naomi said, ruffling his hair. "And baked potatoes."

"I love baked potatoes!" Aaron said. "What's for dessert?"

"Cinnamon buns." She couldn't help but smile down at him.

"I can't wait," Aaron said, and he turned as Claire came inside the house. She shot Mose a smile.

"Mose, I've got a crate of groceries in the back of my buggy," Claire said. "You wouldn't mind carrying them for me, would you?"

"G-groceries?" he said.

"*Yah*, I stopped by the grocery store since I was going that direction anyway," Claire said, and she pulled her wallet out of her purse. "We had to stock up our pantry. Naomi, I didn't write it down yet, but here are the receipts. I also paid our bill at the fabric shop. I took two hundred, and there's some change…"

Naomi's heart hammered to a stop. "You took the money?"

"Took it?" Claire's face pinked. "I did the errands."

"That's what I meant," Naomi said, shaking her head quickly. "I'm sorry. I didn't mean to make it sound that way."

Mose disappeared out the side door, and Naomi put a hand to her chest, her heart pattering beneath her fingers.

"What's happened?" Claire asked. She picked up a fresh apron.

"We thought it was Trevor," Naomi whispered.

"You thought what was Trevor?" Claire asked.

"The money—we thought he took it."

Claire's mouth opened, and her eyes widened. "Oh, no!"

"*Yah*…" Naomi put her hands against her heated face. "I think we've accused him falsely, Claire. Oh, dear!"

Mose's boots sounded on the step, and he came back

inside with the crate of food carried easily in his strong grip. He put it onto the table with a heavy thunk.

"Claire, could you take over in the kitchen?" Naomi asked, her voice sounding breathless in her own ears.

"*Yah*, of course!" Claire was already tying her apron.

Naomi put a hand on Mose's arm, grabbed a fistful of his shirt, and tugged him along after her toward the door. He resisted for a moment, and then complied, allowing her to drag him outside after her. It had been an instinct—something she used to do back when they were children playing together, but the stakes were much, much higher now.

What had they done?

Chapter Eleven

Mose allowed Naomi to pull him after her. At any time he could have tugged free of her grip, but he didn't want to. His heart was still hammering from the realization of what he'd done. He'd all but accused that boy of stealing, and Trevor had been just as innocent as he claimed!

Naomi stopped in the drive, but when Mose looked over at the house, he could see Claire in the window, and he didn't want an audience for this. He'd made a big mistake, and he wasn't going to get the words out with Claire watching them.

"C-come on," he said, and he caught her hand, tugging her after him this time. His mind was spinning, and he pulled her after him, around the stable to where they were out of sight in the lowering evening sunlight. They stood there for a moment, just staring at each other.

"I...accused him," Mose said at last.

"What did he say?" she asked. "Exactly!"

Right. Words mattered here, even if they were hard for him to articulate.

"That the money was for paying some bills for his car. His mother gave it to him," Mose said, his words halting. "He was offended that I'd think he stole it. He knew the people from the grocery store tour recognized him, and he was upset about that."

It had taken a long time to get all the words out, but Naomi waited patiently for him to finish. She stayed silent, then slowly shook her head.

"It was my fault for even saying anything about the money—"

"No!" He caught her hand. "I'll f-f-find him."

He'd make it right. He'd apologize, explain himself. Instead of telling Trevor how to apologize and make things right, he'd show him what that looked like. *Gott* sure had a way of humbling his people.

"Find him where?" Naomi asked, shaking her head. "I don't have an address. I don't have banking information. This was a very informal arrangement!"

Then how was he supposed to fix this? Had he just deeply hurt a vulnerable teen and cut off his connection to a Christian home that might be a good influence on him?

"I was w-worried about your safety first," he admitted.

"I know." She dropped her gaze. "I seem to have dragged you right along into my own games again, haven't I?"

"Not this time," he said. "This is m-my fault."

He'd been the one to go talk to Trevor. He didn't have to do that. It could have waited a day. Mose had been giving in to his feelings for Naomi, and his lack of self-control and his overly protective feelings for this woman had caused even more pain.

"I go home t-t-tomorrow," he said quietly. "I seem to have caused enough trouble anyway."

She nodded. "You and I just seem to fall back in together, don't we?"

Tears rose in her green eyes, and his breath caught. Did she feel that much for him? Would she really miss a stuttering man like him?

"I was g-g-going to write to you," he said.

She blinked. "To me?"

"To explain," he said, slowing the words down to get them out. "And apologize for…everything."

"Oh…for that." She licked her lips.

"Did you want to hear from me for…more?" he asked.

"I thought we were friends again, Mose," she said. "I thought maybe it wasn't just me chattering away at you this time, and it was more mutual."

"It is," he replied earnestly. Friends… Did she have any idea how far past friendship his feelings went? She wasn't his pal, his buddy. She wasn't just a girl who'd been nice to him all those years ago. She was an extraordinarily beautiful woman, inside and out, and he couldn't stop thinking about her.

"Well…" She swallowed. "My sister is going to arrange a marriage for you anyway. I'm sure you'll end up married to Lydia or some other lovely woman before fall is finished. And Lydia is perfectly wonderful—"

"I don't…want that," he said, and as the words came out, he knew them to be utterly true. He didn't want to marry some woman he hardly knew and make the best of it. He didn't want a cordial relationship with a perfectly sweet wife, a houseful of children to stand between them, and have that be enough. He wanted what he felt with Naomi—the stomach-heaving, mouth-drying, anxiety-inducing wonderfulness of being next to her.

"You don't want what?" she whispered.

"S-s-someone else." Mose stepped closer, and he touched her cheek gently. He had so much he wanted to say—like how she turned his world upside down and filled his thoughts constantly. He wanted to tell her that he'd been looking forward to seeing her from before he'd even set sight on her again, and how he loved everything about her from her wild curls to her bright eyes. But that was a lot to get past a stutter, so he took the easy way out and lowered his lips over hers.

This time, he slid his arms around her waist and pulled her close against him. She sank against his chest, and he felt like his heart would pound straight out of his body. He'd never felt like this with any other woman, and in some part of his imagination, he'd hoped that this was possible. And now he had her in his arms, and he had no solutions whatsoever, but she felt perfect right here.

Naomi broke off the kiss first, and Mose let out a shaky breath.

"Why did you do that?" she whispered.

He could just as easily have asked her why she'd kissed him back, because that kiss wasn't one-sided.

"I—" He searched around inside of himself for the words—the exact words. "I…love you."

"What?" Naomi stared at him, her eyes wide, and then they suddenly misted.

"Yah..." He shrugged. "I do."

He worried about her, he cared about her safety, her happiness. He longed to see her, thought about her feelings, about her hopes and wishes. He longed to just stand next to her again and struggle to get his words out, because when she listened to him, he felt like the strongest, most important man in the whole world...or perhaps in *her* world. And that made it even more special. To be the man in her world, protecting her, providing for her...

As if a man with his limitations could even be hoping to be the man for Naomi. She could do so much better than a man who could hardly get his thoughts out of his own mouth.

"We shouldn't be falling into each other's arms like that," she breathed.

"Yah." He knew it well enough, and for some reason after that kiss, his words came out with hardly a stutter. But he still had some illogical flicker of hope. "Unless there's something between us."

Naomi blinked up at him, and then shook her head. "Mose, we don't dare toy with this."

"I'm not t-t-toying." Did she really think he went around kissing women behind stables on a regular basis? She was the only woman he'd ever kissed!

"I don't think you'd be happy with me," she said, her voice catching.

"Because of Klaus?" he asked, the words coming out almost smoothly.

"Klaus?" She smiled faintly. "No, not really. Maybe

he saw what I'm seeing now—that he would have bat-
tled me for the rest of our lives. His rejection stung my
pride, but it didn't break my heart."

"Then?" he prompted.

"I'm..." Naomi touched a curl that had fallen in front
of her eyes, and she plucked at it. "I'm this, Mose! My
hair never stays in place. I'm drawn to making waves in
the community because I want to help *Englishers* more
than most people think I should—more than you think
I should! I have opinions—and the ones you've heard
are just the top of the haystack!—and our community
has all agreed that I'm a wild liberal. I've even heard
people say that if I was left alone, I'd end up Mennonite
within a year and not even realize it. This is who I am,
Mose, and while it's tempting to think I could change
myself at this late stage... I'm old enough to know that
isn't really possible."

Mose looked down at her with those flashing eyes,
and the curl that still hung loose over her forehead. He
wanted to touch it, wrap it around his finger...but he
wouldn't.

"Daniel and Leah..." he said quietly.

She nodded. "Do you know what he told Leah? That
she made him a worse Christian."

Mose blinked. "Th-th-that's not fair."

"It's how he saw it," she said, smoothing her apron.
"He was being honest. I think after two years of a marriage that didn't work, they're at least at the point of
honesty now. Marriage changes people. I'd never considered before that someone might not like what they
became."

Mose had started doing things he didn't think he'd

ever do since seeing Naomi again. He'd brought her an *Englisher* worker, going against the spirit of the bishop's wishes, at the very least. He'd started following his feelings, even when he knew they went against what he'd very logically chosen for himself. This was not what he'd meant to do...

Did that mean he was going wrong?

"You've th-th-th-thought about us together," he said with a small smile.

"Of course!" Naomi looked up at him, her eyes filled with misery. "You came to Redemption looking for a wife, and I... I fell in love with you. How could I not think about it?"

He could think of several very good reasons about why not, but looking down in her face, he couldn't believe he was hearing the words.

"I love you, too..." he said.

"You know I'm not the woman you came looking for," Naomi said. "You told my sister you wanted someone quiet. As much as it hurts for me to say it, I'm not the sweet, conservative woman you were praying for. Let *Gott* answer your prayer for that woman, because if I had to face your unhappiness after you realized what the rest of your life would be like, I don't think my heart could take it. You don't see what it did to Leah..."

"She's in pain..." he murmured.

"She's a shell of herself, Mose."

Did he want to be the reason Naomi lost her sparkle? Did he want to hurt her worse than Klaus had? That thought was like a punch to the gut. She was right, of course. They were both looking for something different, and had found each other. But marriage wasn't just about the courting, or the honeymoon. It was about year after year of working, planning and raising children together. The choice had to be a logical one.

"I wouldn't make you happy, Mose," she said, her voice shaking.

"I would f-f-frustrate you a l-l-lot, too," he said, his throat thick with emotion. "I'd h-hold you back."

Not every Amish marriage was a happy one, and they certainly all began with bright hopes. When he'd worked with the *Englishers*, he used to get frustrated when they figured they could get the results from an Amish life without living one. Well, maybe he wasn't so different right now, hoping for a long and happy marriage, but not making the hard choices when he needed to.

"We need to be...practical," he said.

"Yah." Her lips trembled.

He touched her chin with his thumb, and wished he could kiss her just once more, but his heart could only take so much, too.

They walked together back out in the sight of the house again, and he looked at the smoke twisting up from the chimney, and the kerosene light now shining from the kitchen window.

"I'll leave," he said, his voice tight.

"I was going to feed you," she said, tears in her voice.

"I was g-g-going to love you," he said, and tears welled in his eyes. He couldn't stay longer. And he would not cry in front of her, so he gave her hand one last squeeze, and he headed back toward his buggy. It wouldn't take him long to hitch back up.

Maybe he needed to get Naomi out of his system before he settled into an appropriate arranged marriage. Maybe he had to see why it would never work first.

But as he hitched his horses, he couldn't even imagine marrying any other woman. Naomi had his heart, and even if he'd never be the husband for her, it would take a long time for him to dislodge her again.

Gott, I prayed for a wife, he prayed silently. *Help me to stop loving Naomi. Take away the pain...*

But *Gott* didn't seem to be answering him, because as Mose climbed into his buggy and flicked the reins, he felt like his heart tore in two as the horse headed back up the drive. Maybe he'd loved her all along. But now that he knew it, letting go wasn't going to be easy.

Naomi went into the house and pushed the door solidly shut behind her. Her chin trembled, and she clamped a hand over her mouth to stifle the sobs that would not wait. Claire looked up from setting the table, and her eyes widened in alarm.

"Naomi! What happened?" she gasped.

But she couldn't talk about it, and tears blurred her vision. The house smelled of roasted pork and steamed vegetables. Everything was ready for a perfect meal with Mose tonight, but he wouldn't be eating it.

And somehow, the thought of yet another delicious meal passing by without someone she loved thanking her for her cooking was almost too much to bear. She'd been satisfied with her single life, willing to wait on *Gott*'s timing. And then Mose had landed on her doorstep, and she couldn't quietly wait a moment longer.

Aaron stood in the middle of the kitchen, staring at her in alarm, and the last thing Naomi wanted to do was scare him.

"It's okay," she said, swallowing back the tears. "I'm just going to go wash my face…"

And she stumbled up the stairs, bypassed the bathroom completely, and closed herself into her bedroom. There, she buried her face in her pillow and wept.

She loved him…and that had taken her by surprise. But she did love him. And perhaps she understood Leah's heartbreak a little bit better now. If she foolishly married a man she loved this much, and then couldn't make him happy, the rest of her life would be misery.

She was smarter than this! So why had she let herself fall for a man so obviously not meant for her?

Downstairs, she could hear the soft murmur of Claire's voice in answer to her son's worry. His piping little voice pierced the floorboards.

"Why is she crying, *Mamm*? Why? Is Naomi hurt? Is she sick? Does she need soup?"

Then the soft murmur of words Naomi couldn't make out.

Just like Leah, Naomi wasn't alone. She had people who loved her, who would stand by her, and help her heart heal. But tonight, Naomi couldn't even face the ones who loved her best.

She shut her eyes and let out a slow breath.

Oh, dear Gott, she prayed. *Show us both our way forward. And take care of Mose tonight…*

Because she'd broken Mose's heart, too, and she knew it.

* * *

The next day, Bishop Zedechiah Glick arrived to visit his cousin, Claire. He came inside with a ready smile, and he had a bag with some new books inside for Aaron, too. Naomi didn't feel like herself, but Claire had taken over the bulk of the work, and Naomi had never been so grateful for a good friend in her life. She hadn't told her sister what had happened, either. And she wouldn't—not until she had smoothed her feelings down enough to at least be able to pretend to be happy for the woman who married Mose.

Naomi was grateful for the distraction of washing dishes as the bishop came inside. He squatted down and chatted with Aaron a little bit, and then smiled his thanks when Claire brought him a cup of coffee.

"Someone has been asking about you, Claire," the bishop said.

"Oh?" Claire turned back to fetch the sugar bowl. "Who?"

"I'm not sure...that's the thing," he replied. "Someone in Indiana was asking for a friend who said he'd known you a long time ago, and he wanted to know if the Claire Glick he'd read was doing basket weaving in Pennsylvania was the same Claire Glick he'd known."

"And how would that be narrowed down?" Claire asked with a short laugh. "I don't think I'm very unique in my name or my crafting."

"He knew your parents' names, your sister's name, and your birthday," the bishop said, sobering.

Naomi looked over to where the bishop and Claire stood facing each other. Someone was searching for Claire. Was this an old friend...or someone she wanted to avoid? Claire didn't talk much about her family or friends from her hometown.

"Oh! Well…then I imagine I am the same Claire," she said, but her smile was hesitant. "But who is it?"

He shook his head. "It occurred to me that it might be…" The older man's gaze flickered toward Aaron, and then back to Claire.

Naomi understood the implication immediately. Could it be Aaron's father? Claire had met him during her Rumspringa, before she was baptized. Claire had put off formally joining the church for a couple of years for her own personal reasons, so she was closer to twenty by the time she met Aaron's father.

Claire blanched, and she pressed her lips together.

"Aaron, can you run outside and get me some lettuce?" she asked.

"Yah, Mamm," Aaron said heading for the door.

"Wait!" she said. "Get a bowl!"

Aaron came back to the counter and Naomi held a bowl out to him with a smile. He accepted it and ran back out the side door, letting the screen bounce behind him.

"Why would he search for me now?" Claire asked, growing serious. She looked over at Naomi, including her in the conversation.

"I don't know," the bishop replied. "But I won't reply one way or another without your permission. If it is him, do you want him to know where you are?"

Claire was silent for a moment.

"Does he know about Aaron?" Naomi asked.

Claire shook her head. "He left. I never had the

chance to tell him, and…then I suppose I kept my secret for my own reasons."

"Because you didn't want him to come marry you out of obligation," Naomi said.

"*Yah*. If he didn't want me, then I wasn't going to hinder him."

"He should have come back and married you—obligation or not," the bishop said, then sighed. "Regardless, if this is him, it's your choice, Claire. Do you want to see him?"

"I don't know yet," she replied, her voice shaking.

"That's fair," the older man replied. "Then I won't answer yet."

That was one thing Naomi truly admired about their bishop—his discretion and wisdom. He'd never push a woman into marriage, and he could be counted upon to be gentle in people's lives.

The screen door opened again and Aaron poked his head inside.

"*Mamm*, there's a car here!" Aaron said.

Naomi and Claire exchanged a look, and Naomi wiped her hands. Perhaps it was a tourist stopping by to see what they offered.

"I'll check into it. You two talk," Naomi said, and she crossed the kitchen and took off her apron at the door. She hung it on a hook and stepped outside in the cool, September air.

The car in the drive was a familiar one, and she saw Trevor in the driver's seat and a woman sitting next to him. Trevor was back! She'd given up hope that she'd see him again after she found out what had happened, and her heart skipped a beat. She smiled, took a step forward, but Trevor seemed to be in conversation with the woman, and Naomi stopped short. She watched them, deep in some earnest conversation, and then the doors opened and they stepped out.

Trevor's face was pale and he shoved his hands into his jeans pockets.

"Miss Naomi, I wanted to tell you that I didn't take anything from you," Trevor said, seeming to skip all greetings and niceties all together. "And I brought my mother along to be my witness that that money wasn't stolen. She gave it to me to pay a bill after work."

"I'm Sharon Wright," she said. "Trevor's mom."

The woman stood a pace behind her son. She was a little shorter than he was, slim, and her face looked as pale as her son's did. They were both visibly upset. Her lips were compressed into a thin line, and she looked ready to argue, if need be. Naomi gave her a hesitant smile.

"I'm Naomi Peachy," she replied. "I'm sorry to meet under these circumstances." She turned to the teen then. "I know you didn't take anything, Trevor. I'm so sorry about that. My friend Mose saw me worried about the money and looking for it, and then he saw you with money, and… Oh, Trevor, we are both so, so sorry! You did nothing wrong. And you left so quickly that we couldn't make it right with you."

"If you need that money you lost, we'll give it to you," Sharon said. "We aren't poor, and we aren't thieves."

"No!" Naomi shook her head. "No, we found it. My friend had taken the money to run errands. It's all ac-counted for, and Sharon, I cannot begin to tell you how sorry I am. I know that having your son accused of something would be terribly upsetting. I don't know what you must think of us now, but if Trevor would come back to work, I'll be very happy to have him here."

"So...we're okay?" Trevor said, frowning. "You know I didn't take nothing, and we're good?"

"Yah," Naomi said. "If you'll forgive me, Trevor, then...we're good."

Trevor shot her a lopsided grin. "Thanks. I was really worried."

"Me, too," she admitted. "Trevor, we did hear the rumors about you from those tourists who came by, but here we believe in second chances, and forgiveness. Right now, I'm hoping you'll forgive us, and give us a second chance."

"Uh...sure. Yeah. Sure." Trevor looked rather uncomfortable, but he did cast her another smile. "Is the stable done yet? I could clean it out now, if you want."

It was his gesture, and Naomi cast him a misty smile.

"No, it's not done yet," Naomi said.

"I'll just—" Trevor hooked a thumb in the stable's direction. "Just a quick once-over. It won't take too long, Mom."

"Go, go," Sharon said, and she turned to Naomi. "I was hoping to talk with you alone anyway."

"Oh?" Naomi said. "I hope I didn't overstep in offering to help with his reading. You see, our children stop school in grade eight, but I know that getting through grade twelve is very important for your people, and I was trying to respect that. Even if it might not have looked that way."

"I appreciate that more than you know!" Sharon said.

"I saw it right away—that you were trying to respect what we want for our kids. In fact, I'll be encouraging him to take you up on that offer. I have trouble with reading, too, so…" She shrugged, her face pinking.

"I can certainly help him, if he wants it," Naomi said.

Sharon was silent for a moment, her gaze directed toward the stable. The stable door opened and Trevor came out with a wheelbarrow. He was working quickly—showing off a little—and Naomi smiled.

"He's a good worker," she said. "He's learning quickly."

"When you hired him," Sharon said, "he changed overnight. He came home and said he had a job now and he had to work. Some of his friends who are up to no good called him up and asked him to go out, and before he would have gone. But he said, no, he had to get ready for work the next day."

Naomi smiled. "He's proud of himself."

"But more than that," Sharon said, turning toward her. "He told me that you talked to him, and you treated him like he was worth trusting. He said he was going to do better so that you'd never know about his past mistakes, so when those people recognized him, he was really upset."

Naomi was silent.

"He wants to be better, Miss Peachy. He wants to turn things around, and as his mom, I can't thank you enough!"

"I don't know what I did!" Naomi said earnestly. "I don't deserve thanks!"

"You listened to him," Sharon said, tears in her eyes. "Everyone stopped doing that after a while—teachers, bosses, anyone in any kind of authority over him. But you listened. Thank you for taking him back. I know he'll work hard for you."

"Thank you for letting him come," Naomi said, reaching out to catch Sharon's hand in a firm squeeze. "I'm very happy to meet you, too, Sharon. Maybe while he finishes up, we could get some pie."

"Yeah?" Sharon brightened. "I've heard about your pie."

Naomi and Sharon went inside to chat, and Claire and the bishop took their conversation outside. It was closer to an hour before Trevor had done a quick once-over in the stable, and when he came back to the house, he promised to do a much more thorough job the next day. Sharon and Trevor left with smiles and a plate of baked goods that Naomi had packed up for them to take home.

When Trevor and Sharon had driven away, Naomi turned toward Claire and the bishop, who stood in the shade of the apple tree.

"Bishop, that's our new employee and his mother," Naomi said. "I'm sorry that he's an *Englisher*. I'm not trying to defy orders, but he's the only one I could find to do the work, and..." She wasn't sure what else to say. "And I promised him he could keep working here."

"That's fine," the bishop said. "And I feel I need to ask your forgiveness, too. I overheard your conversation with the boy's mother."

"Oh?" Naomi sifted through her mind, trying to remember exactly what she'd said.

"You made a difference, Naomi," Bishop Glick said slowly. "A big difference. A Christian difference. And

I can see how *Gott* used you with that young man to put him onto a better path."

Naomi held her breath.

"I was very concerned about protecting our own community, but maybe there is a bridge here—a way to reach out and show *Gott*'s love, but to do so more cautiously. I think we may need to revisit that politician's request. We can't do everything they want, but perhaps there's some middle ground. Maybe we can give some classes on how to do farm work, or something. Maybe *Gott* needs our hands in this community more than I realized."

Tears welled in Naomi's eyes. "Bishop, I think that would be wonderful!"

"No promises," he said. "I still need to talk with the elders. But we'll discuss. Seeing you—and that *Englisher* family—I have a different perspective now. Sometimes opposites in relationships can bring out the best in all of us. Not always, but when *Gott*'s hand is involved, it's a definite possibility."

As Bishop Glick took his leave of Claire and said goodbye, Naomi's heart had closed over the bishop's words. Sometimes opposites could bring out the best in each other when *Gott* was involved. And what if, more than just involved, *Gott* was at the very center? Could two opposite people bring out the brightest and best in each other? If there was a bridge between the Amish and the English, was there one available for Mose and Naomi?

Dare she hope?

Chapter Twelve

The bus ride back to Ohio was a long one—nearly eight hours with all the stops the bus made. Mose sat toward the back of the bus alone, his Bible on his lap. He was looking for peace as he watched the farmland melt into towns, which then broke into farmland again as the bus made its way across the countryside.

The *Englishers* had been right—there was a special feeling around the Amish land, almost a tangible sense of blessing there. It wasn't just farmland that lay like a held breath, bated and full of hope. It was Amish land.

Mose's heart still felt heavy and sad. He'd fallen in love with the wrong woman while he'd been in Redemption, and he wasn't sure how he went so wrong on this visit. It was supposed to be simple—help his uncle and start proceedings with a matchmaker. That was it.

If he were giving advice to another man, what would he tell him?

Forget her. She's not the one for you. You'll only waste your time. Write letters with the more appro-

priate woman and look for reasons to love her. You'll find something.

Very logical. But impossible for him to follow, because his heart just wasn't letting go. Love was far from logical, it seemed. Was this how a man ended up single for his entire life? Was this how a confirmed bachelor came to be—with a heart that just wouldn't cooperate?

When he arrived at the bus stop closest to his community, he took his bag and stepped off the bus. He was home, and it wasn't like he didn't have more options now that he was back. He had a matchmaker who had ideas about potential matches for him... His mother would be thrilled about this. And she wasn't going to understand that he couldn't go through with it.

Mose took a taxi to his family's farm, and when he got there, he found his parents getting ready for a hymn sing that was going to be hosted on their property the next evening. Perhaps worshipping with his community would help clear his head. It was the last hope he had, because his heart felt full to the brim with sadness, and his arms ached with emptiness. He'd kissed Naomi twice, and already he never wanted to kiss anyone but her.

He'd let himself fall for Naomi, and it was reckless of him, but it was done. He'd only have himself to blame if he never did get that family of his own he longed for. He knew how his heart worked. He shouldn't have let himself fall for her.

The next evening, before they started singing, their bishop had a short worship, and the sermon was on the passage in Proverbs that talked about protecting a man's well, keeping his water for himself and not letting it spread about.

Drink waters out of thine own cistern, and running waters out of thine own well... Let them be only thine own, and not strangers' with thee. Let thy fountain be blessed: and rejoice with the wife of thy youth.

The preacher spoke eloquently about protecting a home, keeping a marriage united, strong and private. He spoke about fidelity and trust, and the blessing that comes from doing things *Gott*'s way.

The sermon was not helping Mose's aching heart one bit, because when Mose thought about a wife now, she was plump, energetic, and her wild, red curls always sprang free of her *kapp*. And the thought of marrying another woman was impossible. But the thought of Naomi marrying another man was heartbreakingly possible.

Gott, *is Naomi the woman for me?* he prayed in his heart. *I prayed for a wife, and I found Naomi. Was that Your doing?*

As the singing started, Mose spotted Daniel Lantz away from the rest of the group. His expression was grim, and maybe that sermon had stung for him, too.

Mose headed over to where Daniel stood by a fence, leaning against the top wooden rail.

"I heard you went to Pennsylvania," Daniel said.

"*Yah*, I was there for a couple of weeks," Mose replied. His stutter was still there, but Mose pushed past it, forcing the words out, stammer and all. It had been almost two weeks, and yet so much had happened in that space of time. It could have been a year.

Daniel just nodded.

"I h-h-heard about L-L-Leah while I was there," Mose said.

Daniel looked up. "*Yah?* Is she okay?"

"Not really," Mose said, the stutter still strong. "From what I heard, she's heartbroken. Her friends are worried about her. She's a shell of the woman she used to be—that's what I was told."

The words took longer to get out, but this mattered. This had to be said. Daniel dropped his gaze down to his hands, and he pulled off his hat and scrubbed a hand through his hair.

"She's your wife, Daniel," Mose said quietly.

"We aren't happy together," Daniel replied.

"You aren't happy apart, either," he replied. "And neither of you are f-f-f—" The words seemed to lock up inside of him, and Mose had to shut his eyes to regain control. "…free to try again, marry someone else. It's better to work it out, don't you think?"

"I used to be a spiritual man," Daniel said. "I found joy in serving my community and worshipping *Gott*. Then I married her, and I became…angry, a little bit mean, too. I didn't recognize myself. She's so liberal. She refused to bend for me, to change her ways."

"Did you ch-ch-change yours?" Mose asked.

"Too much! And I was in the right!" Daniel shook his head, the sudden fire in his eyes flashing up and then dimming. "Or at least I thought I was. I thought I'd show her how to do things the right way, and that she'd be happier for it. It didn't work out that way. But it scared me when I lost that feeling of being certain of myself, unshakable in my beliefs. Maybe I wasn't so solid as I thought I was."

"Is she a g-g-good woman?" Mose asked.

"Yah." Daniel sighed. "I think I've lost my faith in me being a good man, though."

How did Mose want Naomi to be treated when she finally did marry? She was liberal, too. But the thought of a man pushing down her spirit made him feel downright angry. She deserved to be treasured. And as unbelievable as it might seem, Mose wanted to be the man to do it... No one else would see exactly what he saw in Naomi.

"A g-good man protects his w-wife," Mose said, speaking slowly to get the words out as smoothly as possible. "He provides for her. He comes home to her. He loves her, even when he disagrees with her."

He didn't give up and leave her miserable and alone. Women might be perfectly competent to care for themselves, but they shouldn't have to do it.

"I stopped feeling connected to *Gott* when I married," Daniel said. "I felt like I lost the purest part of my life."

"D-do you feel c-c-connected now?" Mose asked bluntly.

Daniel looked surprised at the question, then shook his head. "No. I can't say that I do."

"So maybe it wasn't Leah that was the problem," Mose said, the words coming easier now, not so many stammers. "*Gott* is not so easily lost. Perhaps *Gott* is expecting you to grow."

Daniel looked out across the field. "I miss her. I admit to that. When I said those vows, I did mean them."

"She's your wife, Daniel," Mose said, pushing past his halting words. "She misses you, too. Maybe it's time to live up to those vows and love her for better or for worse."

Mose could see Daniel's thoughts colliding all over his face. Finally, he said gruffly, "Does she want to see me?"

Mose shrugged. "Only one w-w-way to f-f-find out."

"I thought marriage would be different," Daniel said. "It's so much harder than I thought. A woman is…" He shrugged.

"A whole other person," Mose finished for him, and there wasn't one stammer in those words. They rang out strong, clear, true.

Daniel smiled ruefully. "*Yah*. That covers it. I've been a fool, haven't I?"

"From what I've heard, she's trying to figure out how to build a life on her own now," Mose said. "If I were you, I'd get myself to her door before she manages to do it."

Daniel met Mose's gaze, then nodded. "That's some wise advice, Mose. I think I'll do that."

A loving marriage was possible between those two. Mose could see it. But it would require Daniel to adjust. He'd have to turn to *Gott* like he'd never done before, and learn to be the husband Leah needed. It would take more faith than he'd ever used in his previous, unchallenged life.

And if it was possible for Daniel, was it possible for Mose, too? Mose had a choice in front of him—go back to Redemption and offer his heart and his name to Naomi Peachy, or stay here and play it safe.

No woman was going to fill his heart the way Naomi did, and no matter how many years passed, he was going to wonder how Naomi was doing, and she'd still keep a part of his heart no one else would ever touch. Was that even fair to another woman he might marry?

"T-t-tell you what, Daniel," Mose said. "I'm going to g-g-g—" The word was stuck again, and he took a breath, starting over in his mind. "…go back with you. We can get tickets on the overnight bus."

"You're coming, too?" Daniel frowned.

"Yah," Mose said. He could have said more, but he was exhausted from the effort of this conversation. Yes, he was going back, because Mose didn't want Naomi to figure out how to move on without him, either. He wanted her to look up at him just the way she had the last time he kissed her, every single day for the rest of his life.

A strong and competent woman could live without the man she loved…but a wise man never asked it of her. Her heart was worth more than any challenges that might come their way.

Gott, I love her, he prayed silently. *Grow me into a better man…for her.*

Naomi knelt in the garden, pulling up the last of the pea plants, and throwing them into a compost heap. The pumpkins were still on the vine, and there were potatoes to dig up before the first frost, but today it was simply clearing out the old foliage in preparation for spring.

She was hoping that the chore would clear her mind out, too, but it wasn't working that way. She'd been praying every day since she was a teenager for *Gott* to bring her the man she'd marry, and this was the first time she'd experienced a love that rocked her life the way Mose had.

It hadn't been a very long visit, either! But there was something about Mose—that same sweet friend from childhood had matured into a strong, faithful man. And she'd fallen in love with him. If only she'd been the kind of woman he needed.

Naomi pulled out another tangle of dried vines and tossed them irritably behind her, then she pushed herself to her feet. The sounds of a car on the drive drew her attention, and she turned to see a taxi pulling up to a stop at the house. Naomi shaded her eyes in the golden, September sunlight, and her heart skipped a beat.

"Mose?" she called. "What are you doing back here? I thought—"

She didn't finish what she was saying, but instead hurried across the grass toward him. Her first instinct was to run into his arms, but before she got there, a sobering thought occurred to her. He'd said he was going to find a wife...and maybe he was back to start that process with Adel in earnest.

She stopped a couple of yards from the car and Mose handed some money to the driver, and the taxi started to reverse. Mose smiled hesitantly.

"I thought you went home," she said.

"I d-d-did," he said. He pulled an envelope out and it crinkled between his strong palms. He looked so hesitant, so uncertain, and her heart was overflowing with heartbreak, even still. She was trying to hold herself back, but all she wanted was one more hug from him.

"Oh, whatever!" she said, and she crossed the distance between them and flung her arms around his neck. "Maybe it's another goodbye, but I missed you."

A lump in her throat cut off any more words, and

she blinked back a mist of tears as his strong arms wrapped around her waist, pulling her in close. She could feel his warm breath against her neck, and for a few heartbeats, they just stood there, wrapped in each other's arms. Whoever Mose married, he'd always be special to Naomi.

Mose pulled back, and he handed her the envelope. "I wr-wr-wrote it d-d-down."

Naomi accepted the envelope. It wasn't sealed, and she pulled out a sheet of paper. Did she want to read this in front of him? If it was going to hurt, she might want to read it alone. But he was standing there watching her expectantly, and she let her gaze drop to the page.

Dear Naomi,
I said I'd write, and it's easier for me to say everything I need to say this way. I can't take the chance of my words getting tangled up inside of me when it matters most.

I love you. I said it before, and I meant it with every ounce of my being. I love you. And I know we're different, but I realized something when I went back to Ohio.

I talked to Daniel, and I saw myself in him...

Naomi's breath caught. Yes, that had been her fear all along.

I don't want to end up heartbroken and half a man for the rest of my life because I left you behind. I know I didn't marry you yet, but you have my heart already.

Daniel is going to talk with Leah and hopefully bring her home to Ohio. He's miserable without her, too, and he might have thought he wasn't as good of a Christian with her, but I think he just realized how imperfect he was all along and he didn't like seeing the truth. Well, I'm not perfect, either, and I don't want to make Daniel's painful mistake.

We're different, true, but I believe Gott *brought us together, and us falling in love with each other was no mistake. I think* Gott *can grow us both, make us better versions of ourselves and let us love each other for a lifetime.*

Marrying you would force me to grow, and I welcome it. Because I don't want another day without you. The last one was hard enough.
—Mose

"Marrying me?" she whispered.

Mose's cheeks grew pink, and he caught her hand.

"Are you thinking of marrying me?" she asked quietly, her green eyes sparkling with unshed tears.

He opened his mouth, but he couldn't get the first word out.

"Because something changed for me, too…" she said. "I know we're different, but the bishop changed his mind about us helping the *Englishers* because he saw the difference I made with Trevor."

She told the story quickly of what had happened.

"And I couldn't get the thought out of my head," she concluded. "If there's a bridge between the Amish and the English, why not with us? Because I love you, too, Mose! I love you so much!"

A tear leaked down her cheek and she brushed it away.

"Th-this part I h-h-have to say m-m-myself." Mose swallowed, and while his words were halting, she waited with bated breath, treasuring every single one. "I love you. I want to be your husband, and to take care of you, and provide for you. I want to be the man who lets everyone else know that you're under my care. I want to have children with you, and grow old with you. Please, Naomi... Marry me."

"Do you need me to change, Mose?" she asked, and she held her breath waiting for his answer.

He shook his head. "No. Just love me."

That was easy enough—she was already in love with the man. She didn't need convincing. She knew the man Mose was, and if he could see himself happy married to her just as she was, she would live her life a grateful woman.

"Well?" he said. "W-will you?"

"Yah..." she said, and she sniffled, wiping her face again. *"Yah!"*

"Yah?" He searched her face, and Naomi couldn't think of a better way to express her heart than to raise up onto her tiptoes and lightly kiss his lips.

Mose bent over her, gathered her close against him and kissed her rather thoroughly. Her heart was soaring among the clouds overhead as she twined her arms around his neck. When they pulled back, breathless, she smiled up at him.

"I love you," he said, his voice deep, rich, and not a single halt in the words.

"I love you, too!" she said.

And then the side door opened and Aaron came tumbling outside. Claire stood in the doorway, her face aflame.

"I'm sorry!" she called. "Aaron, get back inside! Now!"

"It's okay!" Naomi laughed, and she looked back at Mose. He shrugged, a smile on his lips. "We've got news, Claire..."

Because after all these years of waiting, she wasn't playing any secret-keeping games until the banns were read. She was marrying this man, and she wanted the whole community to know.

Just as soon as they could arrange, she'd joyfully become Mose's wife.

Mose squeezed her hand, and she leaned her cheek against his shoulder, still feeling an overwhelming sense of awe.

This was it... This was what it felt like when all of her hopes and dreams finally came into agreement with *Gott*'s will. It was worth the wait.

Epilogue

Naomi and Mose were to be married in a big community wedding held on the Knussli farm. When an Amish community wanted to pull a wedding together quickly, they did it! And all the Redemption families pulled together to make Naomi and Mose's wedding one to remember.

The men helped Jake to finish painting his barn so it would be ready in time for the wedding, and the women pulled together with Adel to make sure there would be food to feed the guests. Even Leah and Daniel were coming back for the wedding.

Daniel brought Leah home with him to Ohio, and they had sorted out a lot of their issues. Leah had written Naomi a heartfelt letter telling her how grateful she was for *Gott*'s goodness. She and Daniel understood each other much better now, and they appreciated each other more, too, knowing how painful it was to be apart. Leah was going to be a *newehocker* for Naomi for the wedding, though, and Daniel was going to be a *newehocker* for Mose, too. These were the attendants who stood with the couple. It just seemed right to include them both.

For the wedding, Naomi had two jobs—to sew her wedding dress, and to make her wedding quilt. Claire wouldn't leave all that work to Naomi alone, and neither would Lydia. The three women sat together, stitching for hours on end until both the simple cape dress in wedding blue and the beautiful quilt made of blue bird blocks were complete.

"I knew he was the one for you!" Claire said with a grin. "I knew it when your sister tossed him in your direction."

"She did not!" Naomi said, then she frowned. "Wait…did she?"

Both Claire and Lydia nodded, and then laughed.

"You were the only one who didn't see what she was doing," Lydia said. "To everyone else it was plain as day."

"It's just as well," Naomi chuckled. "I was stubborn."

"She's a good matchmaker," Lydia said. "I'm hoping she finds me a good man one day soon. How about you, Claire?"

"I told you, I'm happy as I am," Claire said, but Naomi wasn't so certain she wouldn't change her mind.

The wedding was held at the beginning of November, when there was frost tipping the grass in the mornings and all the trees were ablaze in red and gold as if they were celebrating this day just as earnestly as everyone else.

Bishop Glick preached on the sanctity of marriage, and when it was time for the vows, Naomi's heart was aflutter. They stood in front of the rows of friends and family, right in the center of the men's and women's benches while the bishop recited the vows.

"Do you, Naomi, take Mose to be your husband, to love and cherish him, to respect and support him, all the days of your life?"

"I do," she said.

"And do you, Mose, take Naomi to be your wife, to love and protect her, provide for her and cherish her, all the days of your life?"

Mose opened his mouth, and Naomi could see the struggle on his face. The audience was hushed, and Naomi could almost feel them all leaning forward, waiting for the words that would make them married. Mose was in front of hundreds of people, and she knew how nervous he was about this day. All the same, her heart hovered in her throat as she waited for Mose to speak his heart.

"I…I…d-d-do," he finally said, and a smile broke over his face as his gaze met hers. "I do!"

The rest was a blur, because Naomi didn't even remember anything else the bishop said during the ceremony. But Naomi felt a pressing certainty that the rest of her life would be spent patiently waiting for words that would matter more than anyone else's. Mose was worth the wait—both in finding him again, and in waiting for him to say his piece.

When the ceremony was over, Mose took Naomi's hand and they walked away from guests a little bit, ducking behind the big white tent that was set up for the guests.

"We're married!" Naomi said, and she looked up at Mose in wonder.

"Yah…" Mose bent and kissed her. "At last."

As they stood together, sharing these first few wondrous moments of married happiness, Naomi's gaze landed on another couple, standing farther away by the fence. It was Daniel and Leah, and they were holding hands, their heads close together. Daniel pressed a kiss against Leah's forehead, and Naomi felt her eyes mist at that tender display of honest affection.

"They'll be okay, won't they, Mose?" she whispered.

"Yah…" Mose's voice was low and warm.

But Mose wasn't looking at the other couple. He was looking at her, and when she tipped her face up, he kissed her lips lightly, a smile tickling his lips. She reached up and touched his smooth-shaven face.

"Starting tomorrow morning, you'll be growing this out," she said, rubbing his cheek. He'd be growing out his married beard, and within a few weeks, she'd never again see Mose with a smooth-shaven face.

Mose chuckled and nodded. "I c-can't wait."

Today was the beginning of the biggest challenge, and the biggest blessing of their lives, and Naomi couldn't wait to begin, either.

* * * * *

Do you want to see how Naomi's sister, Adel, became the town's matchmaker? Pick up
The Amish Matchmaker's Choice
by Patricia Johns,
available now from Love Inspired!

Dear Reader,

I'm looking forward to starting this brand-new mini-series with you, and I hope you'll grow to love this band of single Amish women as much as I do. Sometimes the right man requires a little bit of patience, and these women are about to find out that the wait was worth it!

If you enjoy my books, come by my website and check out my other releases. I also have a monthly newsletter you can sign up for to keep up with my latest releases and get a peek into my world. You'll find me online on Facebook, Instagram, Twitter, and on my website: patriciajohns.com.

Come on by. I'd love to hear from you!

Patricia

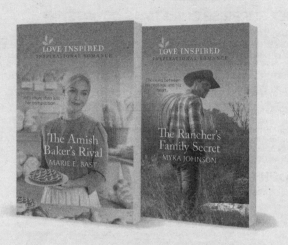

COMING NEXT MONTH FROM
Love Inspired

AN AMISH PROPOSAL FOR CHRISTMAS
Indiana Amish Market • by Vannetta Chapman

Assistant store manager Rebecca Yoder is determined to see the world and put Shipshewana, Indiana, behind her. The only thing standing in her way is training new hire Gideon Fisher and convincing him the job's a dream. But will he delay her exit or convince her to stay?

HER SURPRISE CHRISTMAS COURTSHIP
Seven Amish Sisters • by Emma Miller

Millie Koffman dreams of becoming a wife and mother someday. But because of her plus size, she doubts it will ever come true—especially not with handsome neighbor Elden Yoder. But when Elden shows interest in her, Millie's convinced it's a ruse. Can she learn to love herself before she loses the man loves?

THE VETERAN'S HOLIDAY HOME
K-9 Companions • by Lee Tobin McClain

After a battlefield incident leaves him injured and unable to serve, veteran Jason Smith resolves to spend his life guiding troubled boys with the help of his mastiff, Titan. Finding the perfect opportunity at the school Bright Tomorrows means working with his late brother's widow, principal Ashley Green...*if* they can let go of the past.

JOURNEY TO FORGIVENESS
Shepherd's Creek • by Danica Favorite

Inheriting failing horse stables from her estranged father forces Josie Shepherd to return home and face her past—including her ex-love. More than anything, Brady King fervently regrets ever hurting Josie. Could saving the stables together finally bring peace to them—and maybe something more?

THE BABY'S CHRISTMAS BLESSING
by Meghann Whistler

Back on Cape Cod after an eleven-year absence, Steve Weston is desperate for a nanny to help care for his newborn nephew. When the lone candidate turns out to be Chloe Richardson, the woman whose heart he shattered when they were teens, he'll have to choose between following his heart or keeping his secrets...

SECOND CHANCE CHRISTMAS
by Betsy St. Amant

Blake Bryant left small-town life behind him with no intention of going back—until he discovers the niece he never knew about is living in a group foster home. But returning to Tulip Mound also involves seeing Charlie Bussey, the woman who rejected him years ago. Can he open his heart enough to let them both in?

_____

LOOK FOR THESE AND OTHER LOVE INSPIRED BOOKS WHEREVER BOOKS ARE SOLD, INCLUDING MOST BOOKSTORES, SUPERMARKETS, DISCOUNT STORES AND DRUGSTORES.

LICNM0822

Get 4 FREE REWARDS!

We'll send you 2 FREE Books plus 2 FREE Mystery Gifts.

FREE
Value Over
$20

Both the **Love Inspired®** and **Love Inspired® Suspense** series feature compelling novels filled with inspirational romance, faith, forgiveness, and hope.

YES! Please send me 2 FREE novels from the Love Inspired or Love Inspired Suspense series and my 2 FREE gifts (gifts are worth about $10 retail). After receiving them, if I don't wish to receive any more books, I can return the shipping statement marked "cancel." If I don't cancel, I will receive 6 brand-new Love Inspired Larger-Print books or Love Inspired Suspense Larger-Print books every month and be billed just $6.24 each in the U.S. or $6.49 each in Canada. That is a savings of at least 17% off the cover price. It's quite a bargain! Shipping and handling is just 50¢ per book in the U.S. and $1.25 per book in Canada.* I understand that accepting the 2 free books and gifts places me under no obligation to buy anything. I can always return a shipment and cancel at any time by calling the number below. The free books and gifts are mine to keep no matter what I decide.

Choose one: ☐ **Love Inspired**
Larger-Print
(122/322 IDN GRDF)

☐ **Love Inspired Suspense**
Larger-Print
(107/307 IDN GRDF)

Name (please print)

Address   Apt. #

City   State/Province   Zip/Postal Code

Email: Please check this box ☐ if you would like to receive newsletters and promotional emails from Harlequin Enterprises ULC and its affiliates. You can unsubscribe anytime.

Mail to the Harlequin Reader Service:
IN U.S.A.: P.O. Box 1341, Buffalo, NY 14240-8531
IN CANADA: P.O. Box 603, Fort Erie, Ontario L2A 5X3

Want to try 2 free books from another series? Call 1-800-873-8635 or visit www.ReaderService.com.

---

*Terms and prices subject to change without notice. Prices do not include sales taxes, which will be charged (if applicable) based on your state or country of residence. Canadian residents will be charged applicable taxes. Offer not valid in Quebec. This offer is limited to one order per household. Books received may not be as shown. Not valid for current subscribers to the Love Inspired or Love Inspired Suspense series. All orders subject to approval. Credit or debit balances in a customer's account(s) may be offset by any other outstanding balance owed by or to the customer. Please allow 4 to 6 weeks for delivery. Offer available while quantities last.

Your Privacy—Your information is being collected by Harlequin Enterprises ULC, operating as Harlequin Reader Service. For a complete summary of the information we collect, how we use this information and to whom it is disclosed, please visit our privacy notice located at corporate.harlequin.com/privacy-notice. From time to time we may also exchange your personal information with reputable third parties. If you wish to opt out of this sharing of your personal information, please visit readerservice.com/consumerchoice or call 1-800-873-8635. **Notice to California Residents**—Under California law, you have specific rights to control and access your data. For more information on these rights and how to exercise them, visit corporate.harlequin.com/california-privacy.

LIRLIS22R2

HARLEQUIN
PLUS

Announcing a **BRAND-NEW** multimedia subscription service for romance fans like you!

Read, Watch and Play.

Experience the easiest way to get the romance content you crave.

Start your **FREE 7 DAY TRIAL** at
<u>www.harlequinplus.com/freetrial</u>.

When a wounded veteran and his service dog seek work at the Bright Tomorrows school for troubled boys, can the principal—who happens to be the widow of his late brother—hire the man who knows the past secrets she'd rather forget?

Read on for a sneak peek at
The Veteran's Holiday Home
by Lee Tobin McClain!

Jason stared at the woman in the doorway of the principal's office. "*You're* A. Green?"

Just looking at her sent shock waves through him. What had happened to his late brother's wife?

She was still gorgeous, no doubt. But she was much thinner than she'd been when he'd last seen her, her strong cheekbones standing out above full lips, still pretty although now without benefit of lipstick. She wore a business suit, the blouse underneath buttoned up to her chin.

Her eyes still had that vulnerable look in them, though, the one that had sucked him into making a mistake, doing what he shouldn't have done. Making a phone call with disastrous results.

She recovered before he did. "Come in. You'll want to sit down," she said. "I'm sorry about Ricky running into you and your dog."

He followed her into her office.

He waited for her to sit behind her desk before easing himself into a chair. He wasn't supposed to lift anything above fifty pounds and he wasn't supposed to twist, and the way his back felt right now, after doing both, proved his orthopedic doctor was right.

Beside him, Titan whined and moved closer, and Jason put a hand on the big dog. "Lie down," he ordered, but gently. Titan had saved him from a bad fall.

"I didn't realize the two of you knew each other," the secretary said. "Can I get you both some coffee?"

"We're fine," Ashley said, and even though Jason had been about to decline the offer, he looked a question at her. Was she too hostile to even give a man a beverage?

The older woman backed out of the office. The door clicked shut.

Leaving Ashley and Jason alone.

"The website didn't have a picture—" he began.

"You always went by Jason in the family—" she said at the same time.

They both laughed awkwardly.

"You really didn't know it was me who'd be interviewing you?" she asked, her voice skeptical.

"No. Your website's kind of…limited."

If he'd known the job would involve working with his late half brother's wife, he'd never have applied. Too many bad memories, and while he'd been fortunate to come out of the combat zone with fewer mental health issues than some vets, he had to watch his frame of mind, take care about the kind of environment he lived in. That was one reason he'd liked the looks of this job, high in the Colorado Rocky Mountains. He needed to get out of the risky neighborhood where he was living.

Ashley presented a different kind of risk.

Being constantly reminded of his brilliant, successful younger brother, so much more suave and popular and talented than Jason was, at least on the outside…being reminded of the difficulties of his home life after his mom had married Christopher's dad…no. He'd escaped all that, and no way was he going back.

His own feelings for his brother's wife notwithstanding. He'd felt sorry for her, had tried to help, but she'd spurned his help and pushed him away.

Getting involved with her was a mistake he wouldn't make again.

Don't miss
The Veteran's Holiday Home *by Lee Tobin McClain,*
available October 2022
wherever Love Inspired books and ebooks are sold.

LoveInspired.com